ARCTIC SHOWDOWN

BOOKS BY JOHN BALL

OPERATION SPRINGBOARD

SPACEMASTER I

EDWARDS: FLIGHT TEST CENTER OF THE USAF

JUDO BOY

IN THE HEAT OF THE NIGHT

RESCUE MISSION

ARCTIC SHOWDOWN

John Ball

ARCTIC SHOWDOWN

An Alaskan Adventure

Duell, Sloan and Pearce   New York

DUELL, SLOAN & PEARCE
AFFILIATE OF
MEREDITH PRESS

LIBRARY OF CONGRESS CATALOG CARD NUMBER: 66-13484
MANUFACTURED IN THE UNITED STATES OF AMERICA
FOR MEREDITH PRESS
VAN REES PRESS • NEW YORK

THIS STORY WAS WRITTEN
WITH THE COOPERATION OF THE
UNITED STATES ARMY AND AIR FORCE, ALASKA

CONTENTS

1   *Reunion in Alaska*   *3*

2   *Toward the North*   *14*

3   *Interruption*   *25*

4   *The Coming of Night*   *37*

5   *The Storm—1*   *56*

6   *The Storm—2*   *68*

7   *The Snow Cave*   *85*

8   *Morton*   *100*

9   *Icepick Seven*   *114*

10   *Homecoming*   *132*

ARCTIC SHOWDOWN

1 *Reunion in Alaska*

Andy Driscoll pushed back his plate and rose from the breakfast table. "I'd better get dressed," he said. "Sergeant Ripley is picking me up in about twenty minutes."

"Have a good time, son," his father told him. "I'm going to a staff meeting at Elmendorf, so I won't be here when the sergeant comes. Please pass my regards on to him."

"Sure, Dad," Andy said. He glanced out the window at the strikingly colorless scene and then went to his room, where he had his outdoor gear already laid out on the bed.

He pulled off the light shirt and trousers he had worn at breakfast, and sitting on the edge of his bed, pulled on a fresh pair of long-handled thermal underwear. When he had all of the wrinkles out to his satisfaction, he put on a wool shirt. After that he stepped into a pair of winter trousers and let the shirt hang loosely outside.

Next came the socks. He drew on a light rayon pair for wear next to his skin, and over them an immensely thick pair of white woolen ones. Then he reached for another pair just like them, only one size larger, and put them on too. When he had completed this operation he stood up and walked a few steps to be sure that the soles of all three pairs were smooth under his feet.

Satisfied, he sat down once more and picked up still another pair of the cumbersome socks, one size larger yet, and worked them on over the three pairs which he had on already. Once more he checked that no hidden wrinkles lay in wait to make him miserable outside, but he had done this many times before and the job was perfect. With his feet now unable to feel the floor under them, he prepared to get into his fat-boy pants.

Andy himself was not fat at all. He was trim and well muscled for his age, the result of a good deal of outdoor living, but the fat-boy pants would hide all that. As they lay spread out they looked more or less like a rumpled, many-layered bedspread or comforter. Andy picked up the bulky garment and held it behind himself with his right hand while he pulled the heavy suspenders over his shoulders. When he had them in place, he wrapped the multilayered garment around his hips and legs and engaged the waist-to-ankle zippers. As soon as he had run the heavy-duty sliders down the big tracks, the thick layers of fabric shaped themselves into a recognizable pair of trousers which bulged out so much they made Andy look thirty pounds heavier than he actually was.

With the fat-boy pants in place he sat down—a little less comfortable than before—and reached for his mukluks. Into each of the heavy boots he fitted two pairs of half-inch-thick felt innersoles and made sure that they were smooth. Then he pulled the high-cut boots on over his many pairs of socks, his regular trousers, and the bottoms of the fat-boy pants, checking once again for awkward wrinkles which could become painful later on. Satisfied that everything was in order, he fastened up the mukluks loosely, allowing plenty of air room inside. He remembered the first time that he had put on a pair of these Eskimo-invented foot coverings, how he had fastened them so snugly to make sure the snow couldn't get in and had cut off his circulation. That had been three years ago, when his father had just arrived at Fort Richardson for the beginning of his tour of duty. He had been a little stupid about cold-weather clothing in those days, but no one could say that he hadn't learned.

When Andy stood up, his feet were so thickly padded by so many layers of protection he appeared to be almost two inches taller than his normal height. He pulled a woolen sweater over his head, smoothed it down over his shirt, and then reached for his parka. It was a good one, with real fur around the headpiece, not the synthetic fiber that looked and felt like fur, but which froze into brittle little needles every time the temperature dropped under thirty below—which was often.

Andy trusted his parka. It had proved its value even when the chill factor was down to thirty-thirty (thirty degrees below zero, with a thirty-knot wind) and any exposed flesh would freeze solid in half a minute. He climbed into it and zippered it halfway up over the top of his fat-boy pants. He began to feel very hot, and hurried to finish his dressing. He fitted his fur-lined arctic cap over his head, put on his woolen gloves, over them the mitten interliners, and finally hung his pair of foot-long arctic mittens around his neck by the strong line which guarded them against loss. There was nothing childish about that: if a mitten were to slip down a snow crack and be lost somewhere out in the open, the results could be disastrous. Experienced Alaska hands took no chances, and Andy, who had been well trained, knew enough to follow their example.

He looked about him once quickly to be sure that nothing had been forgotten, and then, properly dressed for the day he had planned, he stepped outside into the biting bright cold. The thermometer at the front door only registered sixteen below; Andy was grateful for that—he had been afraid that it might be really cold when John was scheduled to arrive. Never having been in the north, his friend from California might have found it a bit uncomfortable.

The snow was brilliant and glistening this morning. There was only about four feet of it, but it covered the landscape all the way to the not-very-distant mountains and then continued unbroken right up to their summits. The few trees in sight were all starkly black against the sky; there was no color at all in any direction that he could look.

Andy walked to the edge of the plowed roadway as two vehicles came into view. One of them was a staff car to pick up his father; the other was an enclosed jeep, which would be Sergeant Ripley coming for him. He watched as the sedan drew up and his father, in uniform, hurried quickly out of the front door and into the heated vehicle. A few seconds later the jeep slid to a stop and Sergeant Ripley swung open the door. Andy climbed in front and made himself comfortable for the ride to the airport.

"Tell me about your friend," Sergeant Ripley invited. His breath showed white in the air, but he was fully dressed in Army arctic clothing including white-rubber thermal boots. He was entirely comfortable.

6

"He's a pretty good guy," Andy replied. "I met him down in the south forty-eight when we went to school together. Since then we've written back and forth a lot and once, when Dad was on leave, I had a chance to visit him. He lives in California."

Sergeant Ripley paused at the gate as they drove out of Fort Richardson and then continued on for the short drive into Anchorage. "Has he ever been in cold weather before?" he asked.

Andy flashed him a smile. "Hardly. He's been out of California, of course, but only in CONUS [military abbreviation for the Continental United States]. Do you want to know something? He's never really seen snow, that is, up close. He's seen it several miles away on the tops of mountains, but never to walk up to it and touch it."

Sergeant Ripley, who was a big, powerful man, swung the jeep easily around a corner and smiled a little grimly. "He's going to see it here, that's for sure," he commented. "I hope he has the right gear to wear."

"Don't worry about John," Andy advised. "He's pretty bright, and what he doesn't know, he'll learn fast."

"Still, if he gets off that plane in a California sport shirt, he'll be lucky to make it into the terminal."

Andy glanced at the back of the jeep. "I see you brought some blankets," he said.

"I thought it might be a good idea," the sergeant acknowledged. "I've met planes that came in from the south before."

In a few minutes they reached the Anchorage commercial field, parked, and went to the terminal to await the arrival of John's plane. The flight was on time and in a matter of fifteen minutes the big jet taxied up outside and swung into ramp position. Because of his warm clothing Andy chose to spend

7

the last few minutes outside, where he had a fine view of the whole operation. And, as he expected, John was the first passenger off the plane. He stepped out onto the portable steps, gathered an overcoat quickly about himself and set out for the terminal on the double.

Andy intercepted him a few feet from the entrance. "Johnny, how are you!" he greeted.

"I'm frozen," John gasped. "It's great to see you, Andy, but let's get inside."

Andy held open the door while his friend bolted quickly through and into the heated terminal. "My gosh," he said when Andy joined him there. "I knew that Alaska was cold, but this is ridiculous. How long is this cold snap going to last?"

"It isn't cold—it's warm," Andy answered. "That is, for this time of year. Why, it's only sixteen below."

"Sixteen below!" John repeated. "How do you stand it?"

"Well, we dress for it, that's one thing. Have you got on thermal underwear?"

"I've got on shorts and a T-shirt," John answered. "But I bought myself a flannel shirt to come up here, an overcoat, and a hat. It's the first hat I've ever owned."

"You can get rid of that stuff at our house," Andy advised. "There's some extra room in my closet. I spoke to Sergeant Cummings in supply and he said he'd loan you some suitable gear while you're up here."

"Say, you've put on a lot of weight since I saw you last," John interjected. "They must feed you pretty well."

Andy grinned. "They do that."

"And you're a heck of a lot taller."

"No I'm not, it's the clothing that fools you. Everybody looks taller and fatter in arctic gear. You'll get used to it."

"Right now I'd like to get used to a nice warm lodge or something with a big roaring fire. What do you have planned?"

Andy kept his face straight as he answered. "Well, today is rather special, since there's going to be a demonstration of paratroop maneuvers. About three hundred men are going to jump at the D.Z. [Drop Zone], and I thought you'd like to see it."

"Outdoors?" John asked cautiously.

Andy laughed. "I never saw a parachute jump indoors yet."

John tried a new tack. "My luggage ought to be up by now. Let me get it and then we can go to your place. Maybe you can loan me some long underwear."

"Now you're getting the idea," Andy answered. "Come on, Sergeant Ripley is waiting for us. He has a jeep."

John looked around. "Where is he?" he asked.

"Oh, he's outside—it's too hot in here for him, and to be

truthful, I'm roasting myself. Let's get outdoors where it's nice and comfortable."

"O.K., if you say so," John answered. He reclaimed his luggage and then pushed open the door to the outside. He took three steps forward, then his feet flew out from under him and he landed hard on the seat of his pants.

"Are you all right?" Andy asked quickly.

"I guess so," John replied from where he was sitting on the walkway. "Say, this snow is slippery stuff, isn't it?"

Andy picked up his bag and gave him a hand up. "You've got a lot to learn about the arctic, John, but you'll catch on. Now let's get over to supply and fix you up properly for this kind of living."

By the time they reached the jeep, John was already cold and was holding his hands over his ears. Andy introduced him to Sergeant Ripley and then climbed into the back, so that his friend could sit up front where it might be a bit warmer. He passed up a blanket and advised John to wrap himself up well until they reached the supply depot.

Once inside, John stamped his feet, flailed his arms, and kept putting his hands over his sensitive ears. "I must have goofed," he said. "I bought a lot of things to wear up here that the salesman said would be just right, but they aren't helping a bit."

Andy laughed. "That salesman has probably never been north of San Francisco. Arctic clothing is totally different from ordinary cold-weather stuff used in the south forty-eight. The trick is to wear a lot of layers and to wear them loosely. Three or even two thin layers are better than one thick one. And you don't wear a belt either."

"What do you use, suspenders?"

"That's right, we have to. Arctic pants are altogether too heavy to be held up with a belt. You wouldn't get a dozen steps along before your pants fell down. And remember what I said about looseness, that's important. Tight clothing just doesn't do the trick, you'll find out."

At supply John was issued a heavy canvas bag, six pairs of quarter-inch-thick wool socks, a pair of fat-boy pants, suspenders, an arctic cap, a pair of arctic thermal boots, and a parka. Andy examined the parka in detail, checked the lining, and felt the fur around the headpiece. "It's a good one," he pronounced. "Down south a boy's best friend may be his mother, but up here it's his parka, at least at this time of the year."

"I'm beginning to get the idea," John said.

The supply clerk returned once more, this time with woolen gloves, mitten interliners, and a huge pair of arctic mittens. When these were added to the pile, John shook his head slowly in disbelief. "I really appreciate the Army loaning me all this stuff," he said. "Your father must certainly swing a lot of weight."

"Lieutenant colonels do have a way about them," Andy answered. "But this is standard courtesy for guests who are visiting us. We outfit all of the newsmen, and any others who come through. They don't own this kind of gear and they've got to have it. Of course, all of the local people have their own."

With Andy's help John stuffed all his equipment into the canvas duffel bag. When he had finished, the bag was crammed full. It was both heavy and cumbersome, and he could barely pick it up. Andy took it and swung it expertly over his shoulder.

"How come you rate a sergeant and a car?" John asked.

"I don't," Andy answered promptly. "Sergeant Ripley is a

friend of mine. When he heard you were coming in and knew Dad would be tied up, he offered to help me out. That's his own jeep he's driving."

From the supply depot it was only a short ride to the senior officers' quarters, where Andy's father and others of similar rank were billeted. Still fighting the cold, John hurried inside with his suitcase while Andy followed with the duffel bag of arctic gear.

"We'll be sharing my room if you don't mind," Andy said. "Up here we don't have too much space indoors, but there's plenty of it outside. You can take my word for that."

"I hope to see some of it," John answered.

The telephone rang.

Andy answered it and came back in a few moments with an odd look on his face. "Sit down," he said, "I've got something to tell you."

John sat on the edge of his bed and looked up. "What is it?" he asked.

"That was Dad," Andy explained. "He wanted to ask if you had gotten in all right and I told him you had and that you had your arctic gear. Then he sprang it. A civilian C-47, that's a twin-engined DC-3, is leaving here tomorrow to go all the way up to Point Barrow, at the northern tip of Alaska. There's some extra space on the plane, and if you'd like to make the trip, he can fix it for us to be invited. That's a long flight over some wild and spectacular country. Do you want to go?"

"Of course I do!" John exclaimed eagerly.

"That's what I told Dad," Andy continued. "It should be quite a trip. To be honest with you, I haven't been that far north myself. Before setting out on anything like that you ought to check in and go through the survival school first, but of course there won't be time for that."

"I don't think anything is going to happen," John offered.

"I don't either," Andy agreed. "But then, you can never be too sure about those things. It's always good to be prepared."

2   *Toward the North*

Even with Andy's help, it took John almost an hour to get into his borrowed arctic clothing. To him, everything seemed to be several sizes too large, including the thermal boots, which he regarded as being enormous. "Nobody has feet that big," he said.

"You will, as soon as you get your socks on—all of them," Andy retorted. "And don't try to cheat on the pairs you put on. It's nice outside today, but learn to do it right just in case it gets really cold."

The fat-boy pants were a struggle. Since the heavy-duty zippers ran all the way from waist to ankle, John could not figure out how to put them on, even after Andy patiently showed him several times. "They just don't *look* like pants," he protested. "They don't make any sense."

"Yes, they do," Andy replied. "They're different, that's all. Now try it once more the way I showed you. Forget all about the pants you've been used to."

John followed instructions and at last had them in place. "Now put on your boots," Andy advised.

"I can't," John said. "I can't bend over."

"Sure you can. There are air cells in the boots, so you'll find them a lot smaller inside than outside."

At last John was dressed. He looked at himself in the mirror and said, "I don't believe it."

"Now you look a little like a sourdough," Andy retorted. "Just get used to the idea that life in the arctic is something different. Up here the weather can kill you in a few minutes if you aren't prepared and don't know what you're doing."

"Like getting lost on the desert in the middle of July."

"Exactly. Just do what the old hands tell you and you'll be all right. Get careless, or do something stupid, and trouble can hit you before you know what happened. Now let's go over to the D.Z. and watch the show. Dad will be by to pick us up any time now."

Outside, protected by his arctic cap and surrounded by the protection of his parka, John found the weather much more agreeable. He kicked at the snow a little and tried making a snowball just to see how it went.

"I think I'm going to like Alaska," he said. "Funny, but I'm not cold at all now."

"Your feet and ears are well protected," Andy explained. "That's two places where you usually feel the cold most. You still have to watch your face, though. Here we use the buddy system: I'll watch you for any signs of frostbite, and you watch me. Here's Dad."

Colonel Driscoll's staff car pulled up at the curb and the officer climbed out.

"Dad, you remember John Owens," Andy greeted him.

"Of course. Welcome to Alaska, John. I hope you're going to enjoy your visit here very much. I see you have your arctic gear; how does it feel?"

"Pretty bulky, sir, right now. But I'll get used to it."

"That's the idea. Get in and we'll go over to the drop zone. That is, if you think you'll be warm enough."

"I'll make it, sir." John climbed in next to the driver and watched with interest as the staff car made its way between the heavy snow banks piled up on each side of the roadway. He was looking at a little grove of small trees when he suddenly sat up excitedly and leaned forward, his face close to the windshield. "Andy," he exclaimed, "I think I see a moose!"

Andy took it calmly. "You'll see lots of them, John; they're all over the place. We have to tie down the garbage cans behind the mess halls because of them."

In another fifteen minutes the buildings of the military installation were gone and they appeared to be entering open country. "Look up at the poles along the road," the colonel said to John. "You see those large red globes? They are to warn parachutists that there are phone and power lines below. We'll be turning off into the drop zone in just a minute or two."

Soon the car swung to the right onto a snow-covered, unpaved road, pushed on for a quarter mile, and then halted where a handful of other vehicles were parked, among them a conspicuous ambulance.

Andy took John aside. "We're invited to watch," he explained. "But we're expected to keep out of the way of the brass. That includes Dad." He looked at his watch. "The birds will be overhead in about five minutes. They'll be Air Force C-130's."

"I thought Army parachutists were going to jump," John said.

"That's right. Up here we have a unified command; everybody works together to get the job done."

Within a very short time the whine of a turboprop transport could be heard, and a C-130, flying at only about fifteen hundred feet, came into view. As it reached the edge of the long, level field which was the designated drop area, a row of paratroopers came out of the back, one directly behind the other. A second transport, only a few seconds behind, dropped another stick of jumpers and the sky seemed to be filled with parachutes. Then came a third transport, and a fourth. The first of the jumpers, clad in white outergarments, hit the ground and began to cross quickly toward a wooded area at the edge of the field. Plane after plane dropped its jumpers; one man, who must have hit the ground hard, appeared to have hurt his ankle. From out of nowhere a helicopter seemed to appear. It sat down directly beside him, and two crewmen jumped out. The helicopter paused while the injured man was loaded on board and then took off immediately, turned directly around, and headed back to the main fort area.

"Probably just turned his ankle," Andy said, "but they don't take any chances. He'll be looked after right away."

"Why do you practice parachuting in Alaska?" John asked.

"Dad's the man to answer that, but the experts figure that the arctic is probably the battleground of the future. This is a state, don't forget that, and it might just be the place some future enemy might decide to grab some bases close to the rest of the country. Cold weather won't stop an aggressor any more. In fact, it might help him. So we have to be ready for anything—and we are."

"You know a lot about it," John commented.

"I can't help it, I'm an A.B.," Andy answered, "—an 'army brat.' But don't get me wrong, I like it."

At that point Colonel Driscoll walked up to them and said, "How about some lunch?"

"Come to think of it, I'm hungry," John answered.

"Good; then we'll go and eat."

At the house they were served by a young woman. John kept looking at her, and when she had left the room, he asked, "How did a Japanese girl get up here?"

"She isn't Japanese," Andy told him. "She's Aleutian."

"You mean Eskimo?"

"In a way, yes."

"So there really are some up here?"

"Of course. One of the lead jumpmasters you saw this morning is an Eskimo. And he's all man, believe me. He's a sergeant and one of the best rescuemen in the whole state."

"Boys," the colonel interrupted, "I don't want to interrupt your reunion, but I've got to get back to work in a few minutes and I have some important things to tell you."

He rested his forearms on the table and spoke with quiet authority. "After giving the matter some serious thought, I have decided to let you both go on the special guest flight up to Point Barrow because it is a most unusual opportunity. At the same time I want you to know that I am concerned because John has not had any experience in cold weather and as far as I am aware hasn't been trained in survival techniques. Is that right?"

"Yes, sir—I mean I haven't had any special survival training. I can handle myself pretty well, though."

"I don't doubt that, John," the colonel answered, "but arctic survival requires very special training. Ordinarily I would not let anyone go out on a long flight without clearing through the survival school first; it's a basic requirement. I called your father this morning and talked to him about it. Since the weather looks good and there is no reason to anticipate any problems, he said to go ahead. Now on his authority I'm going to let you go, but if for any reason you find yourselves in any kind of a difficult situation, I'm going to ask you, John, to follow Andy's lead and do exactly what he tells you to—not because he's my son, but because he's lived up here for some time, has had the right kind of training, and has a good deal of experience out in the open."

The colonel paused to judge the impact of his words.

"I understand, sir," John said.

"Good. Now the plane you are going on is a corporation aircraft. I haven't met the aircraft commander, but I understand he is very experienced and reliable. A party of newsmen is being taken up north to see certain installations for the first time; that's the reason for the trip. You'll be up there for one night and then come back the next day. It will give you a chance, John, to visit north of the Arctic Circle."

"I thought we were there now, sir."

"No, not by some distance. That's quite some country up that way. There are no roads, of course, and the only way to travel is either by dog sled or airplane. You'll see a real frontier; most people who haven't been here have no appreciation at all of the arctic and what it means. This trip should really teach you a great deal."

"I'm looking forward to it," John said.

"You won't be disappointed. Now I have to go, but I've arranged with Major Reed at Elmendorf to see that you have a good tour of the Air Force facilities this afternoon. That ought to keep you busy. Get your parkas and I'll drop you off."

The afternoon passed quickly for John and so did the evening, when Colonel Driscoll took them into Anchorage to see the city. John found it disappointingly small and was startled by the generally high prices.

"Practically everything offered for sale in Alaska has to be brought in by sea," the colonel explained. "There's very little industry here. When you realize that you're halfway from the West Coast to Tokyo, and a long ways north, you can see why the transportation costs are high. This, of course, creates higher prices."

"I thought I saw some railroad tracks," John interjected.

"That's right: you saw the Alaska Railroad, which belongs to the government. It isn't connected to any other lines on the North American continent. Any cars from other lines have to be brought up by ferry."

Since the morning departure was to be an early one, and the temperature was sinking steadily, the visit to Anchorage was cut short. Following the brief ride back to Fort Richardson, both boys turned in early, but not until Andy had checked over a small knapsack he had of special survival gear. John was a little surprised at some of its contents. There were balls of heavy twine, two or three knives, a water-purification kit, extra sunglasses with very dense lenses, a few first-aid supplies, elastic bandages, and several items he could not name.

"You don't have any compass," he commented, wondering how Andy could have overlooked an important item like that.

"In the far north a compass isn't any good," Andy explained.

"We're too close to the magnetic pole for it to be useful. There are other ways of finding direction with the sun."

"Why all the string?"

"I'll tell you what," Andy said. "As soon as we get back, I'll ask Dad to set you up for the survival school. You'll like it. It's not all fun, but the exam is a dandy. And then you'll know what all these things are for."

"I can usually handle exams," John told him.

Andy laughed, a little grimly. "This is a different kind of an exam. They take you out into the field and leave you there— on your own. You have a few essential things and that's all. If you get back all right, and haven't starved in the meantime or gotten frostbitten, then you pass. If they have to airlift you out by helicopter, or drop you food because you couldn't make out, then you've flunked."

"In other words, it's for real."

"You can say that again. Now we'd better turn in. We've got an early start to make tomorrow."

The morning was dark and sharp with cold. With Andy's help John dressed in a little less time, tied his arctic mittens around his neck, and walked up and down to be sure that the many pairs of socks he was wearing were without wrinkles.

"We're going to eat in the mess hall," Andy told him. "That will give you a chance for a really good meal before we start out."

"I don't go much for breakfast," John answered. "A bowl of corn flakes is about my speed."

"Not this morning, it isn't. Today you're going to have oatmeal, at least two eggs, sausage or bacon, toast, with fried ham on the side, and potatoes."

"Honest, Andy, I can't."

"Well, you'd better! Survival rule number one is never to

go out into the open without a full stomach of good food. You need it. Up here the military messes are all special high-calorie meals to combat the cold."

In a few minutes a vehicle from Elmendorf picked them up and took them to the mess hall. Andy saw to it that John loaded up his tray with the largest breakfast he had ever faced, took as much or more himself, and made sure that every scrap was eaten.

"After that meal, and with all this clothing on, I can hardly walk," John told him. "Man, I'm stuffed!"

"Good. You're going to eat twice as much as usual up here, so you might as well get used to it. Now we have to report to the flight line, so let's get going."

At the Elmendorf terminal, which was modern and pleasant without being fancy, Andy checked in with operations and was directed toward a small group of people gathered off to one side near a ramp gate. Andy carried his personal survival kit while John handled the small bag which contained their overnight gear. An enlisted man who had charge of the group nodded when they came over and checked their names off on the manifest. "Driscoll and Owens. O.K., that completes the party," he announced. "The bird is ready, so you can board her now through Gate Two. It's the C-47 directly in front of you."

The little group lined up before the exit and began to pass outside. Just as it was John's turn to go through the doorway, he was elbowed aside by a big burly man who had several cameras slung over one shoulder and a tape recorder over the other. John flushed and glanced back at Andy, who motioned him to be quiet.

"I've seen that guy before," he said when they were together outside. "He's always like that. Nobody likes him very much, but he does get most of his work published, so they put up with him. Just ignore him; it's the easiest way."

John, who was still burning a little, got onto the plane and found that one pair of seats was still open. He hung up his parka on a coat rack near the door and motioned to Andy to take the window side.

"Of course not," Andy declined. "I live here, and get out in the open all the time. Besides, I can see just as much from the aisle seat."

"You know, it really isn't daylight yet," John said as he fastened himself in. "It sure takes the sun a long time to come up around here."

"North of the Arctic Circle it doesn't come up at all for weeks. This is the far north, John, and where we're going is farther yet."

Slowly the propeller on the right engine began to turn; after several seconds the engine coughed, threw out a cloud of thick smoke, and then settled down into a steady rhythm. A young man, who was evidently the copilot, came down through the cabin and checked that all the seat belts were fastened.

"Our flight to Point Barrow will be at twelve thousand feet," he announced above the sound of the engine. "Please watch the seat-belt and 'No Smoking' signs. The weather looks good; there's a storm front to the west of us, but we should be well clear of it before it moves in. We'll go via Fairbanks and then directly to Point Barrow. You should have a good view of Mount McKinley about forty minutes from now; it will be on your left. Have a nice trip."

He disappeared through the crew door and soon after the port, or left, engine came to life.

"Well, I just hope this pilot knows what he's doing," the burly man announced loudly.

23

Another newsman turned around to answer him. "Maybe you'd like to get off," he suggested. "I'm sure nobody would mind."

"Hurrah," John said softly to Andy.

"You can't get rid of me that easy," the big man answered in an abnormally loud voice. "I'm the boy who always comes back with the story, remember?"

The plane began to move forward and turned to taxi out to the runway.

"Here we go," Andy said.

John remained silent while the plane taxied, while the engines were run up, and while they turned onto the runway. Then, after a few seconds of waiting, the aircraft moved forward, gathered speed, and lifted off the ground.

"I know this is old stuff to you, Andy," he said finally, "but to me it's some adventure."

"It is for me, too," Andy answered honestly. "Every trip out into the arctic is until you are back home. We're just starting; a lot can happen before we see Elmendorf again."

3 *Interruption*

Because the air was cold and the load on board was relatively small, the DC-3 was able to climb at a good speed. Before many minutes had passed, it had reached its cruising altitude and leveled off for the trip up the central heart of Alaska toward the small community at its northern tip. The sun was up, but it hung low in the sky and offered little promise of warmth and power. When Mount McKinley came into view, it was simply the high point in a long range and was not a very exciting sight.

Because the whole area was very new to him, John spent most of his time looking out of the window at the frozen ground below. He could not see too well because of the wing, but he took in all that he could, even though the landscape had largely settled down to a monotonous sameness. It was broken when what appeared to be a large village came into view.

"That's Fairbanks," Andy told him.

"It's not very big," John commented.

"For Alaska it is. The population is pretty thin up here, and it's a lot thinner where we're going. This is the end of the Alaska Highway. From here on out there are no roads, no signposts, nothing but tundra and wild country."

"Is there anybody at all?" John asked.

"Yes, a few Eskimo villages, some small military installations scattered about, and once in a while a trapper or some other kind of sourdough. But Alaska is so big, you can forget about them unless they get into trouble and then it's up to the rescue boys to step in."

John looked at the vast panorama that could be seen around the edges of the wing. "There sure is a lot of space up here," he admitted. "I can see why Texas is in second place now. I guess it's just too cold, though, to be of much use."

"It's cold," Andy admitted. "But you don't know what cold is until you hit the Big Delta region. There, it gets down to more than sixty below."

"Pretty tough to start a car, I bet."

"Impossible. Say you did get it started; you couldn't run it because the tires would just break off like pieces of glass. At that temperature you can't drive a nail into a board—it won't go. You couldn't live to walk a hundred feet in normal clothes."

"A hundred feet? I think I could," John said.

"A couple of years ago a cook thought that. He tried to get from his kitchen to a supply room ninety feet away. It wasn't even down to sixty below, but it was pretty low. He froze to death going those ninety feet."

"That's hard to believe!"

"I know, but it's true. Extreme cold is just as killing as walking into a bonfire, and you'd last about as long."

John thought about that for a while and then leaned back in his seat to rest. He had had a busy two days and needed time to slow down and catch up with himself. Although the DC-3 was an old and slow aircraft, it was still comfortable and the air was smooth. His unusually heavy breakfast made him a little logy and presently, despite himself, he found that he was catnapping.

He awakened when Andy quietly got out of his seat, walked up the aisle toward the front, and knocked on the crew compartment door. It was opened after a few seconds and Andy spoke softly to the copilot. The crewman looked out one of the forward windows on the right-hand side and returned immediately to the flight bridge.

John, who had been watching Andy, looked out himself and saw that a considerable part of the cowling of the number-one engine was covered with black oil.

Almost at once the voice of the starboard engine began to die away and presently the propeller came to rest, its three blades turned edgewise in the feathering position. The copilot appeared in the crew doorway.

"We appear to have a broken oil line in the number-two engine," he announced. "Under the circumstances Captain Gregory decided it was best to shut down the engine, but we are in no danger. Our other engine can deliver all the power we need to remain in flight and to arrive safely at our destination. We will continue on to Point Barrow. We can have the oil line repaired there and should have no trouble making our scheduled departure tomorrow. We will be cruising at a slower speed from now on and our arrival at Point Barrow will be somewhat later than we had planned."

As the copilot disappeared back through the crew doorway, John turned to his friend. "How much of that was on the level?" he asked.

"All of it, I'd say. I saw the oil leak and told the crew about it; they'd have seen it on their instruments anyway pretty soon. Feathering an engine happens all the time. Well, maybe not all the time, but often enough that it isn't any big sweat."

John was still not entirely satisfied. "Can this thing really fly well enough on one engine?"

"Of course it can, that's the whole point of having two. This is an old bird, but a real good one. Relax and take it easy."

John, whose flying experience was limited, sat back and tried to do as he had been told. Each time that he looked out of the window, however, he saw the motionless propeller and the blackened engine cowling, and the sight did nothing to ease his concern.

He had about decided that the time they had spent on one engine had proved Andy's point when his peace of mind was upset by a sudden and quite sharp gust which shook the plane and caused one wing to rise well above the other. The pilot corrected the plane's attitude promptly, but he had hardly done so before another burst of turbulence shook the veteran aircraft. Almost at once the "Fasten Seat Belts" sign came on. John obeyed, wondering how much rough air could affect their ability to stay airborne on one engine. Andy seemed curiously disinterested; he fastened his belt as directed and then sat back just as though he were sitting in an easy chair at home.

Another gust hit and the whole plane shook with its impact.

"Hey, what's going on around here?" someone demanded in a loud, harsh voice. John looked up and saw that it was the same burly individual who had pushed ahead of him at the gate. The big man got out of his seat and pounded on the crew door with the end of his fist. "Let me in," he demanded, "I want to know what's going on!"

The copilot opened the door and spoke quickly before the man could say a word. "Look, sir, I know you're a guest on board, but we're busy up here and have no time to talk. Now please go back to your seat and fasten your belt."

"Are you telling me what to do?" the big man shouted.

"If you want to put it that way, yes, I am. Now please go back and sit down." He shut the door.

"Hurrah," Andy said softly.

Angrily the husky man in the aisle walked the few steps back to his seat and dropped into it as though he were trying to smash it with his weight. The man who had been sitting next to him turned and spoke. "Take it easy, Gill; getting angry won't get us anywhere."

"When we get where we're going," the man with the loud voice answered so that the whole cabin could hear him, "I'm going to cut that young punk down to size. I asked him a perfectly decent question and he tried to tell me what to do."

"Well, that's his privilege," the other man answered. "He's second in command and he had a perfect right to tell you to sit down."

"Not me, he didn't. Maybe he just didn't know who I am. He'll find out soon enough." He lapsed into an angry silence.

"Is he somebody important?" John asked.

"Of course not. If he were, he wouldn't act like that. He's not a regular reporter at all. He's a free-lancer. He just gets whatever he can and then tries to sell it to someone."

29

"Is that allowed?"

"Oh, sure, some of the best men in the business operate like that, but usually they have regular clients. The better they are, the easier they are to get along with—at least that's what Dad says. You can have this character."

"No thanks," John answered.

He had just finished speaking when the aircraft began to rock heavily. Then it dropped with shuddering impact and refused to steady down.

"Just turbulence," Andy said. "If it bothers you at all, just lie back and close your eyes. It helps a lot."

"About where are we?" John asked, a little tightness coming through in his voice.

"I don't know, but the pilots do. Somewhere over central Alaska, probably in the northern half."

John looked out the window and searched the ground. "I can't see a thing but snow," he reported. "No signs of civilization at all."

"Don't expect any," Andy answered. "This is almost a hundred-per-cent wild, raw country. I'll bet half of it has never actually been explored on foot. Hang on!"

The plane lurched violently, then the right wing dropped and the aircraft began to turn.

"We're going back!" John exclaimed.

"I don't think so," Andy answered. "That hunk of weather must have come in faster than was expected and we're trying to get out of it, that's all."

Once more John pressed his face to the window, but this time he looked up at the sky. The clear, bright-blue expanse with soaring white clouds was rapidly becoming dirty gray with patches that were almost black. Andy leaned over and looked out too.

"Are we in any danger?" John asked.

"I don't think so," Andy replied. "But I do think we may have a pretty rough ride before we're through. We're caught in this stuff good, and it's all around us."

"Then why did the pilots fly into it?"

"I don't think they did. Sometimes it comes up all around you and you can't do anything about it. One minute it looks fine and then before you know it . . . here we go!"

The plane suddenly seemed to have been jerked upward by some giant hand, then was slammed down again. The impact shook the whole cabin and a piece of luggage piled in back could be heard crashing to the floor. The beat of the engine became urgent in tone, and once more the aircraft began to turn. Outside, seemingly sweeping around the horizon, there was a vast roll of black clouds which looked like the edge of some great curling wave.

"Line squall!" Andy said, no longer as calm as he had been.

"Is that bad?" John asked quickly.

Andy nodded his head quickly. "On only one engine it is. We might have to make a forced landing."

"Here?!"

"The pilot hasn't much choice."

The seat-belt sign blinked on and off several times in quick succession. One more mighty gust shook the plane and then it seemed to drop straight down.

"Air pocket?" John asked, honest fright in his voice.

"No such thing," Andy answered tersely. "Down draft. Pull your belt up as tightly as you can." He reached over and helped John.

"O.K.," he continued. "Now hang on. If we do go in, brace your feet hard against the seat ahead of you."

John nodded his head nervously and put his feet into position.

31

The remaining engine roared suddenly and then seemed almost to stop. The crew door opened abruptly and the copilot appeared once more. He shouted so he could be heard. "We are encountering heavy storm conditions. Captain Gregory is going to make an emergency landing and we will sit it out on the ground."

"No, we won't!" the man called Gill shouted back in his loud voice. "I've got something to say about this!"

The copilot ignored him. "Please tighten your belts and prepare for a possible crash landing. We will do the best we can, but it may be rough."

Andy turned to his friend and managed a confident smile. "I've always wanted to be in on a forced landing," he said as cheerfully as he could. "Now it looks like I've got it made. I'm just sorry I let you in for it, too."

"We'll just take it as it comes," John answered. "Don't worry about me."

The engine was almost quiet, and the nose of the plane dropped several degrees. Another mighty gust shook the airframe and one wing swung upward at a sharp angle. The engine roared again and the wing came down once more. Then the plane refused to hold still for even a moment; the closer it came to the ground, the more it seemed to be gripped by the rising storm. Two of the passengers had their heads buried in airsickness bags and the sight made John realize that he didn't feel too well himself. The plane was rocking so violently he could do little more than hang on and wonder how long it would be before it would all be over. He was glad they were going to land, because he knew he couldn't stand much more of this kind of turbulence without becoming desperately sick.

He forced himself to take a quick glance out of the window;

they were closer to the ground and it seemed to be a little darker, but the terrain itself appeared to be tipped up at an angle and turning madly. He quickly shut his eyes to keep the dizzying sight from going directly to his stomach. He pulled out the airsickness bag and held it ready. Just then, Andy took a firm grip on his wrist and said, "Hang on, boy, we'll be on the ground in just about one minute."

Once more the plane appeared to drop several feet, then the nose rose slightly and the turbulence eased off. Once more, John trusted himself to take a quick look out of the window; they seemed to be right above the ground, almost close enough for the propellers to touch. He thought that the snow at least would be a soft surface for landing and then, directly underneath him, he heard a sudden very loud scraping sound as though a great quantity of sandpaper were being drawn violently down the belly of the aircraft. Just in time, he remembered to brace his feet.

The engine stopped and the roar of the scraping sound filled the cabin. The plane began to move slightly sideways; then there was a mighty jerk backward and the sound of tearing metal. The cabin swung around as though on a pivot; abruptly, all motion ceased. There was immediate and almost complete silence. No one spoke and no one moved.

Andy was the first to recover himself enough to speak. He looked anxiously at John, concern on his face. "Are you all right?" he asked quickly.

John nodded, a little weakly.

"Airsick?"

Again John nodded, moving his head no more than was necessary.

At that moment the door to the crew compartment opened and a tall, slender man in a blue uniform stood there. In a swift

inspection, he surveyed the cabin and the nine passengers who were still fastened in their seats. "Is anyone hurt?" he demanded in a voice that carried authority.

No one spoke in reply.

The pilot walked the length of the cabin and had a quick look at each person, then he stood in the middle of the group and composed himself. "Gentlemen," he announced, "I'm Bill Gregory, captain of this aircraft and therefore responsible for our party."

The man called Gill had recovered enough to use his harsh, strident voice once more. "We'll see about that," he declared.

The pilot drew breath, but ignored the interruption. "I'm sure you all want to know what happened, where we are, and how soon we will be able to get out of here."

He paused, but this time no one interrupted him. "When we started out," the captain went on, "a storm front was in the area, but lay well west of our flight path. Instead of behaving as forecast, it apparently gained greatly in intensity and moved much faster than expected. Anyhow, we caught it. As you know, we had already lost an engine with a ruptured oil line. When that happened, we called Fairbanks and told them we were turning back. They advised that the storm was too close, that we couldn't get back in time, and that another aircraft had reported severe turbulence in the area."

The pilot wiped an arm across his forehead, as though to relieve some of the strain he had been through. "We did our best to get around the storm, but on one engine, and with no possible alternate airport available, we were badly handicapped. The storm caught up with us and we saw line-squall conditions ahead. In my judgment, we had no real choice but to attempt an emergency landing. I realized what that meant, but I also knew that a severe line squall can rip an aircraft to pieces."

Another of the passengers spoke up. He was in his late fifties and his arctic clothing did not completely disguise that he was of medium height and slender build. His voice was unruffled, and when he spoke, it carried a quiet note of competence. "You made the only possible decision, Captain, we all agree on that, I'm sure. Can you tell us where we are and what the chances are, if any, of getting out before morning?"

The tall pilot took a firm hold on the backs of two seats before he answered that one. He pressed his lips together, and shaped his words in his mind before he spoke. When he did, he left no room for any doubt.

"I'm going to give it to you straight," he said. "We are down in one of the wildest and most remote parts of Alaska. The aircraft is damaged and beyond repair as far as we are concerned. Normally we could expect rescue planes in the mornnig, but with this storm surrounding us, their job is almost impossible. It may be several days before they can locate and reach us. There is very little food on board, and the heat in

35

this cabin will have dissipated in another few minutes. I'd guess it's colder than thirty below outside."

"Then we're up against it," the quiet passenger said.

Grimly the pilot nodded. "Gentlemen, we are. And we might as well face it—what we have on our hands now is a battle for survival. I just hope we can all come through all right."

4 *The Coming of Night*

As he listened to the pilot's words, Andy's mind was on his friend John, who now was also his responsibility. The prospect of having to spend some time in the open did not dismay Andy. He had often been out on trips with his father and had been through the military survival school, but John was another problem. His friend was not used to cold weather and would have no idea how to protect himself.

Although he did not know their exact position, Andy was certain that they were somewhere close to the Arctic Circle, which meant that gripping, paralyzing cold was already beginning to seize their downed aircraft. In the Far North such cold could be a terrible enemy.

The quiet-voiced reporter spoke up on behalf of the passengers. "Captain, since our situation is clearly serious, please tell us what you would like to have us do."

The pilot answered promptly. "The first thing is to find out what we have in the way of food, blankets, and other resources."

Once more the loud-voiced man took the center of the stage. "Do you mean to say," he began, "that we're just going to sit here and do nothing until somebody else comes to our rescue?"

Andy admired the way the pilot did not permit himself to become riled.

"Since I am not personally experienced in the arctic," the captain answered calmly, "I was careful to get a full briefing before I started out on this trip. That is what the experts advised me to do and it is my intention to follow their instructions."

The big man who refused to remain quiet got to his feet. As he stood in the aisle he bulked very large and his raucous voice seemed to rebound from the sides of the fuselage.

"You don't know who I am, do you?" he declared, pointing his thumb at his chest. "Well, I'm Gill Morton, and nobody's ever been able to push me around. That's why I'm a success—because I get in where everybody else is too timid or pussy-footed to go. While they're being polite, I'm the boy who gets results."

He stopped, but no one said anything.

"Now what we need is a strong leader to get us out of this mess, and nobody can beat me at that. You know and I know that the only reason we're sitting here is because there wasn't enough guts up front to fly through a little bad weather."

"I am the captain of this aircraft," the pilot said sharply, "and I am responsible."

Morton boomed his voice at him. "Sure, they call you captain, but you know you're no real officer, you're just a high-class bus driver; you get paid to sit up there and make this thing go, that's all."

The pilot squared around and faced him. "Mr. Morton, behave yourself! The pilot in charge of an aircraft is called 'captain' exactly like the commander of a ship at sea. And in case you're interested, I'm a reserve officer in the United States Air Force with the rank of major, so if you'd rather address me that way, go ahead."

"All right," Morton roared back, "but you said yourself you didn't know anything about the arctic. Well, I told you I'm a smart man and I can prove it—before we left I looked at a detailed map of Alaska and it showed a lot of places right around here. Now here's what we'll do. I'll take charge of the ground party and see that everyone gets along all right while you and the other driver set out and get us some help. You got us into this, and it's your job to get us out."

"No!" Andy declared in a sharp, firm voice.

Immediately the whole party became still. At that moment John noticed, for the first time, that the cabin was rapidly getting cold; he could see his breath in front of his face.

"Did you want to say something, son?" the pilot asked.

"Yes, sir, I certainly do." Andy stood up and faced Morton up the aisle. "That would be the worst thing we could do," he said. "That same mistake has cost a lot of lives in the past, and if you don't know any better, I do."

Morton brushed him aside. "Sit down, sonny," he ordered. "This doesn't concern you."

Andy did not sit down.

"The first rule of survival," he said clearly and distinctly, "is to stay with your vehicle. You're much easier to find that

39

way. When we don't report in to Barrow, they will know we are down and will be out looking for us. You can't expect to see one or two men from a plane flying over, but you can see an aircraft on the ground."

"Go on, son," the pilot said.

"If any of us go off," Andy continued urgently, "then what will we do when the rescue people get here?" He turned squarely toward Morton. "Those things you saw on the map are just places, like the names of mountains. It doesn't mean that anyone lives there. This is all wild country, and if anybody leaves to try and go somewhere, he wouldn't have a chance."

There was quiet again for a moment.

"I think the boy is right," someone said.

"So do I," Captain Gregory agreed. "In the kind of conditions we have up here, if we sent anyone out, he would face an almost hopeless task and be lucky to get back safely. We were on a flight plan, of course, so there is no need for us to try to get help. They'll know we're down soon enough."

"What's the matter with you?" Morton roared. "You said we had no food, and I don't see any warm blankets. We need help, and we need it fast. If we just sit here, we could be goners while you listen to that fool kid."

The quiet passenger had something to say. "The boy is no fool, Morton; even you should recognize that. I understand that he lives up here and knows these conditions better than we do."

Morton slammed his hand down onto the back of his seat. "I never saw such a bunch of weak-bellied cowards in my life. Now whether you like it or not, I'm taking charge. Nobody's going to put *me* into a jam and then back out of the responsibility."

"Mr. Morton, you are not taking charge," Captain Gregory retorted, his voice rising. "The responsibility is mine, and I will discharge it!"

Morton, his face red, shook his big forefinger at the pilot. When he raised his own voice, he bellowed his words with ear-splitting power. "When we get out of here, I'll have your hide for this! You know why you don't want to go out and get some food and shelter for us: it's because you're plain afraid. You're a coward, that's what you are!"

A passenger who had said nothing until now spoke for the first time. "Morton," he said, "you make me sick. If you were the leader of this group, I think I'd cut my throat. Now shut up if you can and let's get organized as we should."

The pilot looked his gratitude at him. "Thank you, Mr. Bernstein," he said. "Now, what have we in the way of food and other equipment?"

Andy spoke up. "I have a small survival kit of my own," he said.

"What are you carrying?" the pilot asked.

"I have some good twine, two knives and a small hand ax, and some survival rations."

"Have you enough food to take care of yourself and your friend for the next twenty-four hours?"

"Yes, sir, I do."

"Then you keep it, since it's yours. We'll pool the rest of what we have here."

"Yes, sir. Do you want me to help with a survival shelter?"

The pilot thought for just a moment. "No, I think we'll be better off here in the cabin; at least we will have some protection."

"If you don't mind," Andy continued, "John and I will fix up our own quarters. Then we'll be out of your way."

41

"Are you sure you want to do that?"

"Yes, sir, I'm used to it." He stopped long enough to take a quick look out the window. "In fact, we'll be better off. We'll stay close by in case you need us."

"That's likely," Morton snorted.

"If you're sure you'll be safe enough, then all right," Captain Gregory stated. "But don't try anything brave and get yourselves into trouble."

"No, sir. Before we go, could you spare us one of the parachutes in back? That's all I'll need, but it would be a big help."

"If you can use it, take one, by all means. But I want you to check with me in no more than one hour, so that I can be sure you're all right."

"Yes, sir." Andy nodded to John to follow him. He picked up the survival bag which he had had stowed under his seat and walked the few steps to the rear of the aircraft. When John reached for his suitcase, Andy shook his head and handed over the survival bag instead. Then he picked up one of the parachutes, and despite its weight and bulk, swung it over his shoulder.

The latch on the rear cabin door was sprung. Andy pushed against it with his foot, and the door swung partly open. Balancing on the sill, he jumped out into the snow, which was well above his knees. Then he turned and watched while John, a little more hesitantly, followed him.

Andy pointed to a thin line of shrubs and light trees that stood stark and black against the whiteness of the snow. "We'll camp over there," he said.

John looked at him doubtfully. "Wouldn't we be safer and better off inside?"

Andy looked at him. "With that fathead Morton on the

loose? No, we'll be better off out here. I know what I'm talking about, you'll see."

It was bitter cold; John pulled the hood of his parka tight about his face and followed close behind Andy, stepping in his tracks, as his friend slowly made his way toward the spot he had picked. When they had gone a hundred yards, they reached the first of the thin timber. "Now aren't you glad you ate a good breakfast?" Andy said.

John agreed with a nod. "Yes, but we didn't know this would happen," he commented.

"Up here you don't take any chances," Andy answered him. "Make one mistake, like the one loudmouth Morton tried to sell, and it can be your last. Now let's get to work."

Andy looked carefully about him and explored a few feet to one side before he finally picked a spot. "This is it," he announced, and dropped the parachute onto the ground.

"I just hope you know what you're doing," John said, and his teeth chattered as he spoke.

Andy looked at him. "You're not really that cold," he said. "Your clothing is giving you a lot of protection. Just forget how your nose feels, because we have work to do."

He took the survival pack, opened it and pulled out a small hatchet. "First of all, we need a fire," he declared. "See that spot right there? Clear it of snow as much as you can while I get some tinder."

Determined to do his part to the best of his ability, John got down on his knees in the snow and began to brush it away from the exact spot that Andy had indicated. He saw no reason for such a careful choice, but apparently his friend knew what he was doing. After four or five minutes of labor he looked up and saw that Andy was stripping the bark from one of the small scrub trees which appeared to be a variety of pine. With his heavy arctic gauntlets John brushed away the snow until he had a respectable hole in the white stuff which, incidentally, he found to be heavier than he had expected. When Andy came over to join him, he was ready.

Andy dropped down beside him and approved his work. "In the arctic you have to have a fire," he said. "You can't get along without one. So we'll get ours going right away."

"Is that why you wanted to come outside instead of staying in the plane?" John asked.

"One of the reasons," Andy admitted. He took several strips of bark and peeled off the inside layers. These he shredded into small fragments and piled them carefully into a loose pyramid. Then he pushed the outer shells into the snow like a miniature stockade. "Windbreak," he explained. "We have only a few matches, so every one of them is important. The last one could make a big difference in whether we get out of here or not."

Reaching into his survival bag, he rummaged around and came up with a white wax candle. He stuck it carefully into the snow behind the windbreak and then took one match out of a waterproof container.

"Why the candle?" John inquired.

"You'll see."

Carefully, and with a steady hand, Andy lit the candle and let it remain where it was while the flame settled down to a steady light. When it was burning well, he lifted it out of the snow and applied it to the little pile of tinder. It took almost a full minute before a thin pencil of smoke indicated that the wood was catching. When he was sure that the fire was well started, Andy blew out the candle and put it back into the survival kit. "Now do you get the idea?" he asked.

"The candle lasts longer than the match."

44

"Sure. A lot of guys would try to light the fire directly with a match. If it didn't go right away, then that's a match gone and maybe half a dozen more before there's any results. Using a candle is the sure way."

"That's a good trick," John commented.

"It's just one of the things they teach you," Andy responded. "And that brings up something else. We're going to have to work pretty fast, because there isn't much light left."

"At this hour? It's only early afternoon!"

"You forget; this is the arctic, and the days are very short at this time of year."

"O.K., what do you want me to do?"

Andy got to his feet, and after carefully adding a few pieces of bark to the growing fire, took a small stick and drew a rectangle in the snow.

"While I'm getting the wood, I'd like you to clear as much of the snow from inside those lines as you can. Keep at it, but take a rest every two or three minutes as you go. No matter what happens, don't work up a sweat. Up here moisture is a worse enemy than the cold. So keep dry; got it?"

"Whatever you say."

"Good." Satisfied that the fire was all right and that his friend knew what to do, Andy took his small hand ax and began to gather pine boughs, cutting them off from the bottom side so that they would not split and peel the bark. He made several trips back to his chosen campsite, carefully adding a little fuel to the fire each time and checking on the slow but willing work John was doing.

When he was satisfied with the branches he had gathered, he cut down several of the small trees, and dragged them back to the center of operations. There he stripped three of them of all boughs until he had three poles. Then he cut the longest of them in two, and in the bare space which John had made, laid out a rectangular framework on the frozen underlayer.

"What's next?" John asked.

"Take the parachute over away from the fire and open it up," Andy directed. "Just pull the rip cord. Then spread it out."

"For a signal, I see."

"Good guess, but not this time; that parachute is going to be home away from home in just a few minutes."

"Thin silk? That can't be very warm."

"It'll do when we get through with it."

John couldn't imagine what Andy was planning, but did as he had been asked while his friend cut down several more small trees and made poles from their trunks. He saved all of the boughs and kept them in a growing pile not too close to the fire. While John was still wrestling with the awkward parachute, Andy thrust six of his poles into the snow at an angle and then bent another over to form a sort of arch. Going back to his survival kit, he pulled out the stout twine and began to lash the slanting poles to the curved one, which was five feet back from the fire. When this work was done, he went back for one more pole, and laying it flat in the snow, lashed both ends of the curved piece to it for added security.

"How are you doing?" he called over to John.

"I've got it out open and spread out. At least I think I have; it's kind of tough to handle."

After checking the fire once more and adding a little more fuel, Andy went over to inspect the result, taking with him a knife from his survival kit. Satisfied with John's efforts, he began to cut the silk canopy along one of the seams from rim to center. When he had finished, he counted out fourteen panels and then cut once more. This done, he cut loose the

46

shroud lines so that he was left with the silk segment and no more.

With John's help he carried the big piece of fabric back to the framework which he had built and stretched it over the top. It covered the poles nicely and left a good deal of material over at the sides.

"Just right," Andy said. "I've done that once or twice before, but this is the first time I came out on the button."

"Say, that's not a bad tent," John admitted.

"It isn't finished yet. Over where I was cutting wood there were some loose rocks. Don't carry too much at once, but it would help if you'd put some of them around the edges to hold the covering down."

"I get the idea," John responded quickly, "leave it to me."

As soon as he had started off, Andy began to select some of the lighter pine branches and laid them carefully on top of the orange-and-white parachute cloth. He did not attempt

to make a complete cover, but only scattered them thinly over the surface. Then he glanced toward the sky to measure the remaining light and went back to the parachute, where he cut off another piece, approximately the same size as the first. By the time he had this done, John had ringed the initial covering with stones and it was firmly in position.

With John's help, Andy carefully lifted the new piece of material over the first. The two layers were separated by a few inches by the scattered pine boughs.

"That ought to be fairly warm," he said when he stopped for breath. "The idea of the branches is to make a dead air space between the two layers; that's one of the best heat insulators there is. Now we can put the rocks on top of both layers, and we're in business."

"I'll take care of that," John offered.

"Good, because I've still got something else to do."

Once more Andy went back to his cutting area and took out two more small trees. When he had pulled them back to the shelter, he dropped them with a sign of relief. "That ought to be all of that for tonight," he said a little wearily. "Are you getting hungry?"

"Now that you mention it . . . ," John began.

"Well, hang on a little while and let me get this done first. The light's going fast, and it isn't easy to work in the dark."

With his hand ax he cut two poles into four-foot lengths.

"Nice-looking firewood," John said.

"Guess again," Andy answered. He laid two of the short lengths out in the snow and then several others across them in the form of a miniature raft. With his twine he lashed them together until he had a small platform. Then he set it up behind the fire and with two of the remaining pieces propped it into almost vertical position.

"That's a fire reflector," he explained, his voice suddenly tired. "It'll throw the heat right into the tent opening. So it oughtn't to be too bad. We'll have to take turns keeping he fire going. Now let's make up the bed."

"Is that what that framework is for?"

"That's right; we'll pack it with the boughs we have left and it won't be bad at all. After that we can eat."

Under Andy's direction John helped haul in and pack the pine branches, all facing the same way, inside the simple rectangular framework. The fire reflector was working, and soon John was ready to shed his parka.

"You sure know how to set up light housekeeping in the wilderness," he said.

"The Eskimos taught us all," Andy admitted. "And the troops in the field have had a lot of experience. Our Alaska boys can be comfortable anywhere. Every time we have mid-winter maneuvers our gang has a fine time while the trainees from the south forty-eight are miserable—they get frostbitten and everything else."

"Why don't you show them the right way?"

"We do, but they don't believe it, so they have to learn the hard way."

"I want to ask something," John interjected. "Why did you pick this exact spot for our camp? You seemed to take a lot of time making up your mind."

"Well, for one thing," Andy answered, "I wanted to be sure that the entrance to our tent would be across the wind. A lot of tenderfeet build their tents and igloos with the entrance into the wind and that can be worse than being outside. Another thing, I wanted to be sure our fire wouldn't be under a tree. Can you guess why?"

"The sparks might fly up and ignite it?"

Andy smiled. "Nope, it's so the heat won't melt the snow on the branches. If that happens, down it comes and puts out the fire or caves in the tent."

"There's a lot to this survival business, isn't there?"

"Well, it sure makes a difference whether you've been taught anything or not. A lot of guys have died because they didn't know where to find food or how to protect themselves with what they had."

John reached over with his gloved hand, scooped up a handful of snow, and put it into his mouth.

"Spit it out," Andy said sharply.

John did as directed. "I'm thirsty," he said. "What's wrong with that?"

"You'll just dry yourself out, that's what's wrong. It takes a lot of heat to melt snow, a lot more than ice. If you eat snow, you'll use so much heat you'll be a lot worse off than before. We'll melt some snow right away, but never try to eat it, no matter how thirsty you get. In an emergency, melt it with your bare hands."

In the dim light Andy produced a small pan from his kit, packed some snow firmly into the bottom so that it would not burn, added two or three stones to the sides of the fire, and put the pan on the ledge which they formed. When he had finished he crawled into the parachute tent and lay down on the pine-bough mattress which he had constructed.

"I wish we had some sleeping bags," he said. "The plane is supposed to carry them when we cross open arctic country. But I don't think we'll freeze if we keep the fire going."

"You've done a terrific job," John responded. "This is actually comfortable."

"You may not think so before we get out of here. If things get too rugged, we may have to build a snow house. But this ought to be all right for overnight. In the morning the rescue crews will be out, and they'll find us, don't worry."

John had nothing to say to that, and for a little while neither of the boys spoke. The only sound in the arctic stillness was the gentle crackling of the fire, which, thanks to the reflector, threw enough heat into the improvised tent to bring it up well above freezing temperature.

Presently Andy rummaged once more in his survival kit, produced a little package of soup cubes, and added two of them to the melting snow in the pan.

"Up here try not to drink anything cold," he said. "Keeping warm and keeping dry are the secrets of surviving. If you take a cold drink, it makes your body lose some of the heat it needs."

"Someone's coming," John cut in. Andy looked up and saw that a lone figure was slowly wading through the snow from the direction of the downed airplane.

"I guess I'm in trouble," Andy confessed. "I promised to check with the captain after an hour and I forgot to do it."

"It's too late now."

As the man came closer, Andy recognized the copilot he had seen several times while the flight had been in progress. He was walking with slow deliberation and seemed to be picking out each spot in the snow before he put his foot down and took another step forward. Since it was not very far from the aircraft to the site where Andy had pitched his camp, the copilot did not take too long to arrive in the shadow of the fire. He paused without speaking and John could see that his face was blue with the cold.

"You're frozen," Andy said. "Come in and warm up. We'll have some hot soup ready in just a couple of minutes."

With an effort the copilot bent down and crawled into the paratent. As he did so, Andy noted that he mostly used his left arm and turned a little gingerly as he sat down. Without saying anything more, Andy pulled a drinking cup out of his survival kit, poured some of the hot soup which was just beginning to simmer into it, and handed it to the flyer.

The copilot took it and carefully raised it to his lips.

"Hot," he said, and then sipped cautiously from the edge of the cup. No one spoke until he had downed half of the steaming liquid and appeared to find his voice.

"Captain Gregory asked me to come and see how you were. We saw your fire and assumed you were doing all right."

"We are," John said.

"How did you hurt your arm?" Andy asked simply.

"In the landing," the pilot admitted. "I got banged against the side of the fuselage when we skidded."

"Did you do anything about it?"

"I couldn't. If I'd used my head, I'd have looked at it right after we landed, while the plane was still warm from the heaters. When it began to hurt, it was too cold and I didn't dare take my parka off."

Andy answered by crawling out and tossing two of the pine boughs onto the fire. They caught almost at once, and the reflector returned the increased heat into the improvised tent. "You can risk it now," Andy said. "Is there a first-aid kit on the plane?"

With John's help, the copilot began to get carefully out of his parka, favoring his right arm as he did so.

"There is," he answered, "but things aren't too good over there. It's gotten awfully cold, and Captain Gregory had a bang-up fight with that man Morton. The rest of the passengers had to separate them."

"Have they any food?" Andy asked.

"Yes, that was what the fight was about. Morton is a big

eater and he had a couple of box lunches with him. Captain Gregory insisted that all food supplies be pooled and shared equally, but Morton wouldn't stand for it. He claimed it was his foresight that he had brought the lunches, and he wouldn't give them up."

Andy turned once more to his kit. "I don't have too much," he said. "This isn't supposed to be a complete outfit, just a supplement to add to the regular stuff."

"I'll go and get the first-aid kit," John volunteered. "I'm not afraid of Morton."

"Don't do it," the copilot advised. "It isn't worth it. Captain Gregory has things under control, but only just. If you show up, it might just start another mess. Morton is a wild man right now and he isn't safe to be near."

Andy produced a small box and opened it. It was so packed with first-aid material that not a bit of space was wasted. "I'll see what I can do," he said.

"I'd sure appreciate it," the copilot replied. "Incidentally, my name's Jim Hill."

"Glad to know you. Now roll up your sleeve."

"I don't think I can."

"Then unbutton your shirt. It isn't really too hot in here, but you'll be all right for only a few minutes."

With John assisting, Hill managed to get half out of his shirt and to expose his right arm. Andy looked at it and then whistled softly. It was swollen from the elbow to the shoulder, and there was an angry black bruise which must be very painful. Carefully Andy ran his fingers over it and then had Jim press each of his fingers separately into his palm.

"I don't think it is broken," Andy said, "but that's a whale of a bruise. All I can do is bandage it for you to keep it from swelling any more. When we have some hot water, I'll put some compresses on it for you."

Jim Hill hesitated. "I'd appreciate it if you can spare the bandage to tape it up," he said, "but never mind the compresses. Bill Grgeory needs me, and I'd better get back there."

"You're welcome to stay with us and keep warm," Andy offered.

"Thanks a lot; I wish I could." He held out his arm while Andy began to wrap it expertly with a rolled-up bandage he had taken from his first-aid box. "We're trying to get the emergency heaters going, and I want to help out if I can."

"If that doesn't work, you have plenty of gas and you can build a fire," Andy commented.

Hill hesitated for a long time. "We won't be able to do much of anything until Morton comes off his rampage," he said. "He's so bull-headed he just won't cool down."

Andy was a little grim. "Up here he's bound to do that."

Hill allowed himself to smile. "I see your point; but he's a terror and no mistake. I've got to get back now. I'll tell the captain that you're all right."

With John's help he got back into his shirt and parka.

"Care for some more soup before you go?" Andy asked.

The copilot paused for a second. "Do you have enough?"

Andy waved his arm as best he could in the confines of the paratent. "We haven't run out of snow and firewood yet, and until we do, we can make lots of it. I have a good supply of cubes. It's a little thin, but warming. I'm sure we have enough until the rescue boys get here for us in the morning."

Jim Hill looked down and seemed to be studying the bulging folds of his fat-boy pants. When he faced Andy once more, there was a different expression on his face.

"I don't think we're going to be able to count on that," he

said. "The captain has been keeping this to himself, but I think you're entitled to know."

He looked outside the tent and peered up at the blackened sky. "When we were flying west of here, we caught the incoming edge of a bad arctic storm," he said. "In two or three hours it will hit us here on the ground. It could be sooner. The last advisory we got told us to execute an immediate emergency landing. You know what that means, don't you?"

Slowly and thoughtfully, Andy nodded.

Outside a sharp gust of wind shook the paratent and whipped the flame of the small fire until it was in danger of going out.

John felt the heavy silence and looked at his friend. "So we're in for trouble, is that it?"

"Tell him," Andy advised.

"I don't know too much about the arctic," Hill admitted. "In fact, this is my first trip up here. I do know what Fairbanks told us. We can expect severe storm conditions for probably the next four or five days."

Another surge of rising wind caught the tent and for a moment threatened to pull it apart.

"We can't look for any rescue planes for the next several days," the copilot went on. "That means we'll have to hack it on our own, and the only food we have is Morton's box lunches. They won't last long."

John understood fully now and he looked at Andy with real fear rising in his eyes. "Can we make out?" he asked.

Andy waited a while before answering.

"I'll do the best I can," he said finally, "but you don't realize what an arctic storm is. If a good one of those hits us, then you'd better face it—our chances will be almost nil."

5 *The Storm—1*

John watched as the young copilot made his way slowly toward the now frozen hulk of the downed aircraft. He could only see him briefly by the light of the small fire; the sky was fully overcast and showed nothing but solid blackness overhead. "I wish he could have stayed with us," he said.

Andy shook his head. "He would have been welcome," he replied, "but I don't think Gregory can spare him." He produced two cups from his emergency kit, pulled them apart, and filled them with the remains of the hot soup. Immediately he refilled the pan with fresh snow and put it back over the fire.

"Drink up," he advised. "With what's coming now, we can't afford to rest any more. There's too much to do."

John sipped some of the hot broth and felt better immediately. It ran into his stomach with a revitalizing warmth and seemed to release fresh energy that his body had been holding in reserve. "What's next?" he asked.

Andy swallowed some soup before he answered. "We've got to get a lot more rocks to try and hold down the edges of this tent," he said. "Then we'll have to cut some of that light timber and prop up the framework against a heavy snow load. That stuff can pile up awfully fast, and what we've got isn't very solid. Also I've got to build some kind of protection for our fire. If that goes out, we've had it."

It was far from easy in the dark. Following his own trail in the snow, Andy made his way back to where he had discovered an area of loose stones. In four laboring trips he and John carried back enough good-sized ones to anchor the edges of the tent so that it could withstand almost anything but gale-force winds. From the available timber Andy cut props by firelight and fitted them into place under the stringers which formed the roof of the tent.

When this was done, John discovered that he was beginning to breathe very hard and the first signs of perspiration were noticeable. He told Andy, who directed him at once to lie down in the tent and to stay there until the cold had settled his body down once more to normal. While he was lying there, looking up at the thin parachute silk which was their protection against the coming storm, he began to have serious doubts that, despite what they had done, it would last until morning.

"Wouldn't we be better off in the airplane?" he asked. "Silk is pretty weak stuff, and the plane is a big hunk of metal that isn't going to cave in or blow away."

Andy squatted beside him, resting from his work for a moment. "That's one of the things they teach you," he answered.

"An aircraft down in the arctic gets so cold you freeze inside, and you can't heat it. We're a lot warmer in here, and don't worry about that silk; it's tougher than it looks."

"I guess you know," John conceded.

Andy shrugged his shoulders. "Look in any survival manual, it's in all of them."

"Then those guys in the plane must be mighty cold right now."

"I'm sure they are."

"Can't we do something to help them?"

Andy seemed suddenly to be thoroughly tired out. "It's too late for tonight," he said. "In the morning maybe we can, but only if they want us to. That isn't our party, and if they wanted us, they would have said so."

John stretched out on the pine-bough mattress and found it to be quite comfortable. "You go to sleep," he suggested. "I'll take the first watch feeding the fire. I've got the idea now how to do it—keep it small and steady."

"Only if you agree to call me in two hours," Andy answered, "and sooner if anything at all happens that looks like trouble."

"Count on it," John replied.

Andy said nothing more. He lay down on his side, looked around once to be sure that all was well, and closed his eyes.

Outside another sharp gust of wind shook the tent, but it was firmly anchored now, and John felt a new confidence that it would hold out at least until morning.

Inside the aircraft it was as still as death. Most of the nine men who were sleeping there, or attempting to sleep, were huddled closely together for warmth. Over themselves they had spread whatever clothing they had been able to find in the various suitcases on board as substitutes for blankets. Only

Morton was by himself, and he was the only one awake. His teeth chattering and his face blue with the cold, he sat in his seat, his arms folded over the two box lunches which he had brought on board. As soon as the others had surrendered to hunger and cold and had fallen asleep, he had begun to eat; and most of one was already gone. In his utter selfishness he had violently refused to share what he had, and the others, in disgust, had, for the moment at least, let him have his way.

In the cockpit Captain Gregory sat in his left-hand seat, wretchedly miserable in the biting cold. He tried every few minutes to slap himself with his arms to keep himself warm; he did not dare to go to sleep because of Morton, who he knew was awake. Beside him Jim Hill, also close to the breaking point, was speaking in a soft, quiet voice.

"You know I'm not questioning your authority, Bill, but that's how it stands. That young fellow was raised up here, and he knows the score better than any of the rest of us. If you don't buy it, go over there and let them feed you a little of their hot soup; they have lots of it."

"You're killing me," the pilot said.

"Of course there's Morton," Hill went on. "But I'm for physically restraining him in the morning, if it comes to that. We can't let one man foul up everything for all the rest of us."

"I'll do it if I have to, but that's an extreme measure I'll avoid if at all possible."

"Well, regardless of Morton, we're sitting here slowly dying, while those two youngsters out there clearly know the answers, or one of them does, anyway. It's like being on top of an overcast with your radios out—when you see a hole you thank the Lord and come down through it."

As Hill finished speaking, the whole airframe shook under the buffeting of the rising wind. Hill peered out of his frost-

covered window and saw that the glow of the campfire was still there.

"Why don't you go over there and see for yourself?" he suggested. "If Morton tries to start anything, I'll raise holy hell and eight of us will jump on him if we have to."

"Why did I have to be cursed with a man like him on this trip anyway?" Captain Gregory complained. "What did I do to deserve it?"

"Forget Morton. You can go out the baggage door; after all, it's your duty to see that they're all right, isn't it?"

"Hot soup . . ." the aircraft commander said slowly through lips that were numb with cold.

"Beat it," Jim Hill said. "Maybe Morton will go beserk and run off in the snow."

"If he does, don't try to stop him—at least not very hard," Gregory said grimly. He got out of his seat with an effort and, so cold that he could hardly move, made for the small door on the left-hand side of the fuselage.

John was still standing watch when he saw the figure coming through the snow. Automatically he looked at the gently steaming dish of hot water, reached for Andy's package of soup cubes, and dropped two in. Then he shook his sleeping companion.

Andy was awake almost at once and looked a silent question.

"Company," John said.

Andy sat up and watched the approaching man who was leaning hard into the strong and mounting wind. As the aircraft commander came close to the fire, Andy said without ceremony, "Come in."

The pilot, who appeared almost exhausted from his short walk, crawled into the paratent and made an effort to retain his dignity. "Are you all right?" he asked.

"Yes, but you're not," Andy answered. "Your face is frost-bitten."

"I don't think so," the captain answered, "I'm not in any pain."

"In the early stages you can't feel it," Andy retorted, "but there are gray spots on your skin, and that means trouble."

"I'll rub it with some snow," Gregory said.

"Sit down," Andy directed. "If you do that, you'll only make it a lot worse. I've seen a lot of guys in the hospital who tried it. Have you eaten tonight over there?"

"We're saving our rations for the morning," the pilot answered without looking at him.

Andy did not wait to ask any more questions. Instead he washed one of the cups out with snow, filled it with the steaming soup, and handed it silently to the pilot. "It's hot—be careful," he warned.

With shaking hands Gregory raised the cup to his lips and took a small sip. Meanwhile Andy produced a fresh handkerchief from a zipper pocket, folded it into a pad, and dipped one side in the hot pan of liquid. Carefully he applied it to the frozen part of the aircraft commander's face.

"You can expect this to hurt a little," he said, "but take it from me, it's the only way to do it. When you're frostbitten, your skin is frozen; rub it and you'll just tear up the little blood vessels underneath and wreck yourself."

For the next five minutes, while Captain Gregory gradually drank the hot broth, Andy kept applying the hot compresses to his face. Once or twice the pilot flinched a little from the pain, but he did not cry out and accepted the treatment in silence. He drank his soup as soon as it was cool enough for him to swallow and accepted a second cup when it was filled for him without his asking.

Outside the tempo of the wind continued to rise. The cloth of the paratent whipped angrily, but thanks to the weight of the stones holding it down, it showed no immediate signs of blowing away. The snow could be seen in whirling gusts close to the fire, but beyond that the night was black and biting cold.

Presently Gregory pressed his fingers experimentally against his sore face and felt the spots which Andy had thawed out. They were tender and painful, but the danger of damage was gone. "If I was this badly off," he said, "I'm worried about the condition the others are in."

"How is Jim's arm?" John asked.

"What about his arm?" The aircraft commander gave him a quick, sharp look.

"It's badly bruised," John answered. "Andy fixed it up for him with what he had."

"He didn't say anything to me about it." Captain Gregory paused for another drink of the warming soup which had done much to revive him. "He didn't want to give me anything else to worry about, I guess."

"Do you know how to tell frostbite?" Andy asked.

"Frankly, no."

"Look for gray or white spots on any exposed flesh. If any of the passengers appear that way, you'd better send them over and I'll do what I can."

The pilot paused for just a moment. "You know a lot about the arctic," he said, making it a question.

"The Army puts most of the dependents through survival school," Andy replied. "And then I've been out with Dad a lot—on camping trips and things like that. I like this country, and I've tried to learn about it."

For another moment the captain paused as though finalizing

a decision in his mind. When he spoke, it was as though he were reading from an operations manual.

"There are two facts I cannot overlook. One of them is that we are down here, considerably off our flight path, and are likely to be stuck for several days. The other is that of all of us, you appear to be the only one who is qualified to direct survival procedures. As soon as it is light once more, would you like to take over and see what you can do to improve our situation?"

"I'd be glad to," Andy answered simply. "Under your authority, of course."

"We'll work it out. You might be thinking about it, because another day of this without some form of protection, at least like you have here, and the rest of us will wind up in serious trouble. Now I'd better get back before this wind becomes any worse."

"Have you got a flashlight?" Andy asked.

"Yes, if it isn't frozen."

"If you need us, flash it from the window. We'll see it."

"I'll do that. Good night."

"Good night." The pilot crawled out of the tent and stood up beside the fire. He looked at it for a brief moment and then, leaning heavily into the wind, began to make his way back toward the aircraft which was invisible in the blackness.

The sky was just beginning to show the first streaks of gray when the sleeping men in the downed aircraft began to awaken. With the exception of Morton none of them had had anything to eat for almost twenty-four hours, but in large part they accepted this without complaint. Nothing could be done, and this was clear to everyone. Morton himself was deep asleep, his arms still closed over the hoard of food he was determined not to share.

Jim Hill woke everyone up, Morton last, and told them that the captain wanted to talk to them. Just before he went over to the big troublemaker, someone asked, "Shall we take his boxes now?"

"Let him keep them," the man called Bernstein answered. "I think I'd choke on anything he gave." Jim Hill prodded Morton, none too gently, until the big man was fully conscious. His first act was to tighten his grip on his boxes of food; then he hefted them to be sure that they were still as heavy as when he had fallen asleep.

In as businesslike a manner as he could manage, Captain Gregory came into the cabin from the cockpit where he had been on watch, and stood up before them.

"I want to come right to the point," he said. "Is everyone fully awake?"

Everyone was.

"Very well. There is a heavy storm outside. It isn't snowing now but the wind is very strong, and conditions are severe. Flying is out of the question. Do you understand what I am saying?"

Preston Williams, a nationally famous reporter with a quiet voice, replied for them all. "In plain language, Captain, there is no hope for any immediate rescue attempts."

"I may be wrong," the pilot answered, "but the only thing for us to do, as I see it, is to assume that we may be here for several days and to prepare for that."

"I don't think I can last that long," one of the reporters said, with a touch of fear in his voice.

"That brings up what I want to talk to you about," Captain Gregory continued. "When we checked last night, there was no one here with any arctic experience to speak of or any knowledge of this part of the world. During the night I learned differently. You all remember the two boys who were with us and who went off to camp by themselves."

"Are they all right?" someone asked.

"I would certainly say so; I visited them last night after everyone else was asleep, and they were far better off than any of us. They were reasonably comfortable, they had a warmed tent, and, if you'll forgive my mentioning it, they provided me with some welcome hot soup."

"You didn't give us any!" Morton roared. His loud voice was like a shock wave in the cabin, made more so by the fact that he had not spoken previously.

Gregory turned toward him. "You were well provided for, Mr. Morton," he said icily. "You retained your own supply of food and refused to share it, so I saw no need to consider sharing anything with you."

"So I'm being discriminated against, is that it?" Morton sneered at him.

Gregory ignored him. "Gentlemen, all of us want to get out of this alive, and I think we are all aware that our situation is serious. By a stroke of good luck we have someone in our party who, in my judgment, can increase our chances of survival materially if we choose to follow his lead and his instructions."

"You mean that boy who lives up here," a previously silent reporter said.

"Exactly. I am thoroughly convinced he knows what he is doing, and he is the only one among us who does. I propose that I will retain nominal responsibility for our party, since that is my job, but that we ask him to take charge of our survival efforts. That youngster is no fool, you can take it from me, and he is thoroughly trained in arctic conditions."

"I'll second that," Jim Hill contributed. "I visited him and his friend too."

"Did you get some soup?" someone asked, a bit grimly.

"I did, and if we ask him, I'm sure he'll produce some for all of us. How about it?"

There was only a brief pause; it was broken when Morton spat out an unprintable word. "I can take care of myself," he added, "and I've proved it. You gutless wonders wouldn't have empty bellies now if you were in my class." Deliberately rubbing it in, he opened the upper box which he held and took out a small piece of fried chicken. Making sure that everyone was watching, he put it between his teeth and bit down. The click could be heard throughout the cabin. The burly man bit harder, his jaw muscles straining, but it was useless. He thrust the chicken leg back into the box and pulled out half a sandwich. When he tried to take a bite, it too was frozen as solidly as a piece of ice.

A dangerous ripple of laughter ran through the frozen, hungry men. Morton's face became livid as he had to face their ridicule, then he thrust the frozen sandwich inside his parka.

"I'll thaw it out next to my skin," he said through his teeth. "I was going to share this morning, but since you guys chose to laugh at me, now you can go hungry."

Bernstein snorted, and then spoke to the captain. "I don't see any other way," he stated. "I'm certainly not too proud to learn from somebody else, and the fact that it's a boy doesn't bother me at all."

The captain looked about him. "Is that the consensus?" he asked.

"No," Morton barked.

"I would say *yes*," Preston Williams returned. "If Mr. Morton does not choose to join us, that is his privilege."

The captain looked about him, but no one else spoke. "Then it's settled," he announced.

He turned to his copilot. "Jim, it isn't pleasant outside, but would you go over and ask that young man if he would come here and assume direction of our survival program? The way things are now, I'd say he's the only chance we've got."

6　The Storm—2

Jim Hill found it tough going from the aircraft over the scant hundred yards to the place where Andy and John were camped. The unceasing wind seemed to be blowing with gale force, and the paratent was whipping madly. Around the fire area Andy had piled up enough snow to protect the small blaze and it was still going well despite the fury of the lashing wind. When the copilot reached the shelter he crawled quickly inside and fought to recover his breath.

"The captain wants you," he said to Andy. "I don't know if you want to try going over there in this wind; it's pretty tough."

Andy answered by closing up his parka and pulling on his arctic gauntlets. John prepared a cup of the ever-present hot

68

liquid from the fire, dropped in a little snow to cool it quickly to drinking temperature, and handed it to Jim without a word. The copilot drank it down and then stopped to shake his head sharply as though trying to clear away cobwebs. "You'd better make some more," he said. "It's going to be needed."

"We only have one pan," John answered. "If we can get something else that will do from the plane, then we'll make more as long as the cubes hold out."

"Let's go," Andy said. He crawled out of the tent, leaned into the whistling wind, and began a slow, steady walk toward the aircraft. Jim followed behind him, and at the pace Andy set found it a little easier to get back. The hot liquid in his stomach had revived him and the hunger pangs were not as sharp as they had been. When they reached the aircraft he motioned to Andy to go first and then followed him inside.

"So here's the boy wonder," Morton said.

Captain Gregory wasted no time. "Andy," he began, "it's clear to all of us, with one exception, that our situation is very serious. We're pretty close to frozen, we have no food, and none of us has had any experience in arctic survival procedures. You have. We've talked it over and have agreed—we want you to show us what to do."

"I'll do the best I can," Andy answered.

"All right; then let's put it that way: insofar as survival measures are concerned, *you* are in charge. Mr. Morton, who has his personal food supply, has chosen to go his own way; the rest of us are all with you."

Morton got to his feet. "I've got something to say," he announced in a voice which, for once, was not a bellow. "It may surprise you to hear this, but I agree with the captain here that our situation *is* serious. But when things like this occur, good common sense is the best asset you can have. Now I've got a lot of that and you know it. And if I do say it myself, I've got a lot of drive and that's what we need right now. So I'll make you all a proposition. We need a strong leader to get us out of this, and the boy here obviously isn't it. If you want to elect me your leader, right here and now, I'll not only guarantee to get us all out of this mess, I'll start out by splitting up the food I was the only one smart enough to bring along. Now you're all hungry, and I've got enough to give everybody something to eat; we can thaw it out at the kid's fire over there. This is your first and last chance; how about it?"

"Have you had any experience in the arctic?" Captain Gregory asked.

"I've had experience in every part of the world," Morton answered. "The arctic is no different. It's cold, sure, but that's all. I've made out all my life, and I told you last night, I get in where everybody else is too afraid or too pantywaist to go." He raised his voice automatically until it was booming. "In plain language, I've got guts and that's what we need here."

"What would you do, Gill?" someone asked him.

"Well, first of all we're going to eat. I'll pitch in what I have and then the kids have hot soup, we've all heard about that, and we'll all be better off. Then we can start a fire right here in the airplane to keep warm. There's plenty of things we can burn."

"Including the airplane," Bernstein cut in. "It's made of aluminum, Gill, you know that, and aluminum burns."

Morton cut him off. "That's a detail and you know it. Now this is your last chance, am I your leader? How about it, heh?"

"I don't think so," Preston Williams said. "Personally, I have more confidence in the boy. And he was smart enough to bring along a few things he might need too."

"I agree," another man said.

"We'll take a vote to settle the matter," Captain Gregory said. "You all know that leading this party is my responsibility. I propose to delegate the survival part to this young man here who has proved, to me at least, that he knows what he's doing."

"Trying to weasel yourself some more hot soup?" Morton sneered. "Come on, fellows, don't fall for that kind of bunk."

"All those in favor of Mr. Morton's assuming command of our party," Captain Gregory said coolly, "raise their right hands."

Morton shot his own arm into the air and looked expectantly at the others. One reporter half raised his hand and then pulled it down again. "I guess I'm not *that* hungry," he mumbled.

"Those in favor of my plan," the captain said. This time the timid reporter raised his hand bravely, but he need not have done so. Only Morton was opposed.

"All right, Andy," the captain said. "What do you want us to do?"

"There isn't much doubt what we need, sir," Andy answered. "In order I'd say food, shelter, heat, and a method of attracting help."

"I offered the food," Morton said sharply.

"I think I know where there is some more," Andy continued. "Do you carry life rafts on board?"

The captain nodded. "Yes, they're standard equipment. We have two of the twenty-man kind."

"Then we have provisions for the next few days; every twenty-man raft includes a supply of rations; it's part of the gear."

"You're right!" Jim Hill cut in. "I knew that, but I'd forgotten it."

"Then I'd suggest that you lay out the rafts on a clear place and unroll them. Do it in that little grove of trees where they won't blow away. The wind is always much less even in a thin stand of any kind of timber. Put some rocks in them to keep them down. Take out the food kits and give them to John. He'll thaw them out at the fire, and as soon as possible, everyone will get something to eat."

A general murmur of approval came from the near-frozen men.

"We have a good fire going and will supply everybody with warm water to drink."

"At least that isn't any problem," one of the men said.

"In the arctic it can be a severe problem," Andy answered. "People who haven't been trained try to eat snow and it only dehydrates them instead. Snow is a lot harder to melt than solid ice, so don't try to eat any. Is there any coffee or tea on board?"

"We do carry some instant coffee," Jim Hill said. "Normally we have a little coffee-making setup, but it isn't working."

"We can make the coffee," Andy replied. "Not a lot all at once, but we'll keep everyone supplied in rotation."

"I'm beginning to feel better already," Bernstein said. "If any help is needed with the life rafts, I'll be glad to lend a hand."

"That would be a good idea," Andy answered. "If you feel like it, I'd suggest that you and Mr. Hill start right away. Next, I'd like to ask how many knives or hatchets there are on board."

"Knives?" Captain Gregory queried.

"Yes, sir, the Eskimos have a saying that in the arctic with a knife you can survive, without one you need a miracle."

"I have a pocket knife," a reporter volunteered. "It's not much of one, but you can have it."

"Good," Andy said, "are there any more?"

No one spoke.

"We may need some more help with the rafts," Jim Hill cut in, "they're pretty heavy, and the snow out there is deep."

"Take off the cabin door," Andy advised. "It's curved and will make a good sled. You can pull the rafts on that."

"I'll help," a reporter said. It was the timid one who had almost voted for Morton as leader. Now, clearly, he was out to make amends. The three men got up stiffly, but with the prospect of something to eat and a definite task to do, they pulled themselves together and went to work. One of the orange-colored rafts was secured in the tail of the aircraft; they rolled it out and then started to remove the passenger door.

"Next," Andy continued, "we ought to lay out a parachute as a marker; it's much easier to see than an airplane on the ground—the color stands out much better than a plane. I don't know if we can do it in this wind, but as soon as possible we ought to mark our location."

"How about my doing that," the captain volunteered.

"Fine, sir, then why don't you take the man who has the knife with you. When you get the parachute laid out, weigh it down with snow blocks or anything you can get. Cut off the shroud lines and save them; they'll help build shelters. I'm going to try to snare some game."

"That's likely up here," Morton said, sneering.

"There are rabbits and some other small game," Andy answered patiently. "And there are moose. That's another proposition, of course, but if we need food we can try to get one."

The aircraft commander walked to the rear and shouldered a parachute. "These things can be useful, even on the ground," he said. "I can see that."

"While you are out there, sir, you might tramp out the symbols for 'food and water' and 'damaged aircraft.' Do you know them, sir?"

73

" 'F' for the first one and two right angles facing each other for the second, I believe," the pilot answered immediately.

"Yes, sir, that's it. You know how big to make them. If they come over, they can use the spread-out parachute for a D.Z."

"I don't have a job yet," Preston Williams said.

"We need a signal fire," Andy answered. "One that will send a good column of smoke into the air. I cut a lot of boughs last night that we can use. If we can drain some gasoline out of the plane and saturate them, it will help to get it started in a hurry if we hear any rescue planes. That's a two-man job, so you had better take someone with you. If the wind is too bad, it can wait."

"No, I don't think that it can," Williams answered. "A lot might depend on it. I'll do the best I can. Maybe Sam Welles will help me."

Welles was quick to respond. "I always did want to be a boy scout," he said. "Now, by golly, I've got my chance."

"Do you want to help, Gill?" Williams asked.

"No," Morton replied tersely. He was in a foul mood and it was evident to everyone.

Andy turned to the two men who remained. "We're going to need a lot of timber for shelters and firewood. Would you like to help me cut it?"

"Helping with something that is going to result in getting warm will be a pleasure," one of them said. "What will we use for tools?"

"I have a hand ax," Andy answered. "We can take turns."

Outside, the weather was brutal. The cold hit like a blast because of the biting wind; overhead the lightening sky was obscured by a very low deck of ragged black clouds which was sweeping ominously across the shallow valley in which the wrecked aircraft lay. A haze of fine, icy snow swirled in the air and stung viciously whenever it hit exposed flesh. Breathing was hard and taking even a few steps was exhausting.

Andy made his way back to the paratent and checked with John, who was miserable. The little fire was no longer able to offset the force of the storm and he was hard pressed to keep the pan of melting snow warm. For a moment Andy allowed himself the luxury of coming inside. "I was planning to build some more parashelters," he said. "But with this wind going, I don't think it can be done."

John, who was too cold to talk, merely nodded.

"I've got something else in mind," Andy went on. "It will be a lot of work, but if it comes off, we'll be in a lot better shape."

"I'll help if I can," John said through his chattering teeth.

"You may have to, I'm going to need all the help I can get."

Andy left the tent and began to plow his way painfully through the snow toward a small rise which was perhaps a hundred feet high. Across its top the wind whistled with relentless power, the feeling of desolation was almost total, and there seemed to be nothing whatever to offer the least hope of shelter. At the base of the rise a massive snow drift almost fifty feet high had accumulated and stood like a great hostile barrier to any human beings seeking to live outdoors in the arctic at this time of year.

Andy stood for several minutes studying the giant drift, and then turned to face the full fury of the powerful storm. He saw the three men who were struggling to bring a rubber life raft across the snow and motioned them in his direction. Then, at a slow, energy-conserving pace, he made his way toward them, his breath coming shorter with each step. When he reached them he spoke up immediately.

"This storm is worse than I thought it was," he admitted. "Leave the raft there." He looked at Jim Hill. "Can you make it back to the plane?" he asked.

"I'm sure I can," the copilot said. Of the three men he seemed to be in the best condition.

"I need a shovel, any kind of a shovel," Andy said. "Look and see if you can find anything that I can use."

"There's a little short-handled spade on board," Hill answered, almost barking the words into the wind.

"I need it badly," Andy shouted back. "And anything else that can be used as a shovel, even a flat piece of metal."

"Anything else?" Hill asked, the snow stinging his face and forcing him to close his eyes.

"How hard is it to get a cowling off an engine?"

Hill hesitated. "Normally it's easy. Do you need one?"

Because it was so hard to talk, Andy nodded his head. "If you can."

"We'll try," Hill shouted back slowly. Andy could see that

the men were willing, but they were desperately cold and they had had nothing to eat for more than twenty-four hours. Nevertheless, they turned and began to make their slow, painful, wind-plagued way back toward the aircraft.

As soon as he saw them started, Andy turned into the wind once more, and conserving his strength carefully, worked his way, one plowing step after another, toward the spot where Captain Gregory and his helper were trying to spread out a parachute in the impossible wind. Andy was almost upon them before they saw him and stopped work to see what he wanted.

"This won't work," Andy panted out. "Wind's too strong. No chance. I need help over here. Please come."

He turned and began to fight his way back, stepping in his own tracks; the two men came behind him without a word. When he had gone halfway he stopped and pointed to the base of the huge drift, where his own would-be helpers were sitting miserably in the snow. "Meet me there," he directed. Then he struck out once more to the spot, only fifty feet away, where Preston Williams and Sam Welles were trying, without success, to build a signal fire. Andy stopped them and led them, too, over to the base of the massive accumulation of snow. When he got there, one of the men who had gone to the plane was back with a small, short-handled spade in his hand.

Andy gathered the men about him in a tight little knot so that he could be heard above the howling wind. "We have to have shelter and get out of this wind," he said. "Other things will have to wait. I can't make tents and keep them up in this wind. I can't build fires."

"Shall we go to the airplane?" Captain Gregory asked. For the first time there was a sagging in his voice, an indication of lack of confidence.

"No," Andy shouted back. "We'd freeze there. There's a way out, but it will take a lot of work."

"What do you want us to do?" Preston Williams asked. He was close to exhaustion, and his even voice was beginning to fail.

"You and Mr. Welles go to the tent and take a ten-minute rest. Drink some soup if we have any. Then come back. We'll all take turns."

Williams looked at Captain Gregory, who nodded. Without protest the two men who were most in need of help turned wearily toward the paratent and the slender comfort it offered. The fire, despite the windbreak Andy had constructed, was whipping to the point where its heat was almost totally dissipated.

Andy took the spade and while the others watched waded well into the snowdrift. When he had gone as far as he could, he chopped straight down into the snow and for two or three minutes worked at cutting a straight vertical wall. When he had cleared away a flat area facing him, he turned around and came back. "Our only hope now is a snow cave," he said. "We can make one in that drift. It means tunneling it out, but there's a way to do it. We'll have to take turns digging."

"I'll start," Bernstein offered.

Andy handed him the small spade. "We want a four-foot hole straight into the drift, starting where I cut a vertical face," he said. Bernstein took the inadequate tool without a word and walked into the drift. He marked a circle on the face of the snow wall and then began to dig.

"Jim Hill is getting a cowling," Andy told the others. "As soon as it gets here, we'll use it for a sled to haul out the snow. It won't be easy, but whatever you do, don't get wet."

One of the men who had gone to the airplane panted his

way toward the party carrying a piece of sheet metal in his hand. "Jim took this off the baggage compartment," he said. "He thought it might be used as a shovel."

Andy seized it gratefully. "It will be just right for cutting snow blocks. Like this." He chose a clear spot, pushed the metal into the snow four times at right angles and then, clearing a place with his gauntlets, cut once from below. He lifted out the cake of snow and set it carefully before the entrance to the snow bank where Bernstein was working.

"The rest of us can build a windbreak," he said, forcing out the words against the lashing power of the near gale. "As soon as it's up, we can make a fire. Snow is a good insulator."

The cold and famished men, under his direction, began to cut snow blocks. Andy took each one as it was delivered and placed it carefully to form a good-sized circle around the growing opening where Bernstein was laboring away. When Williams and Welles came back from the paratent, Andy sent him off to get some hot broth while the timid correspondent stepped in to take his turn. The opening was now full-sized and extended back into the snow a good four feet. Andy looked at the drift and then indicated that the work was to go on. "We need to go ten feet, at least. Somebody please help to get the snow out of the way."

Bernstein returned and the block-cutting continued until the windbreak wall which surrounded the cave opening was a full two tiers high. Andy was just placing the last block into position when Jim Hill, almost at the end of his endurance, staggered up with half of an engine cowling in his hands. He dropped it silently and sank down into the snow. Andy looked at Bernstein who was a big man. "Take him to the tent," he directed. "Get some hot stuff into him if we have any, and let him rest."

As he spoke, a second man, the last of the three who had gone to the plane, also far gone, dragged himself to where the work was going on and released the second half of the cowling, which fell into the snow. He remained on his feet, but swayed a little and seemed to be somewhat dazed. Andy looked quickly at the captain. "He's frostbitten," he said, "you know what to do. Use all the broth if you have to, but thaw this man out and leave him in the tent. He's got to rest."

Gregory nodded, and slipping the man's right arm across his own shoulders, led him away.

The reporter who had been digging came out pushing a small pile of snow before him. "I'll take the next trick," Andy said, and then looked up as John joined the party.

"I've been taking it easy too long," John said. "I want to go to work."

"Then it's us," Andy answered. "I'll dig and you haul the snow out on a section of the cowling. It's a good container and snow sled. Will the rest of you please keep cutting the blocks; when we're four high, I'll start the fires."

Andy took the spade and crawled into the short tunnel. The second man had been willing, but he had not dug well; with the spade Andy smoothed off the sides and shoveled the loose snow onto the half-cowling which John had pushed behind him. Then he attacked the fresh snow in front of him and bored the tunnel steadily forward. He did not come out until the cowling had been filled and emptied several times and the tunnel was a good ten feet long. When he at last emerged, the snow-block windbreak had grown materially and the loose snow from the cave had been piled outside it to add more strength.

"The next two men go and get some soup," he said.

"No, it's your turn," Captain Gregory countermanded.

"You've done a man's work and more all morning. You take a rest and tell us what to do while you're gone."

Someone had had the forethought to bring some firewood to the area and from it Andy selected a short thin stick. With it, he drew a plan in the snow. The others gathered around to watch.

"This is the main entrance tunnel," Andy said. "It's dug now as far as we need to go. The windbreak out front will keep the entrance clear and will be our watch station. We'll have fires there as soon as we can get them going."

At the end of the tunnel he had indicated he drew a circle. "Here's where the work starts—this is going to be the main room at the end of the tunnel. Make it one big step, or a short snow ramp, higher than the entranceway. It should be round, about five yards across, and eight feet high in the middle. That's a lot of snow to take out, but we can do it; as soon as it is big enough inside, most of us can work in there and we can have a little fire for heat and light."

"Inside the snow?" someone asked.

"That's right, as soon as we have a roof vent in, and that won't be hard. At least we'll be in out of the wind and the chill factor will be much lower."

"We'll start on it," Captain Gregory said. "Now go get some rest. If you fold up on us, then we're all finished."

Too tired to argue, Andy returned to the paratent. One of the two men inside was applying hot compresses to the face of the other, who was wincing in agony. "I know it hurts," Andy sympathized, "but whatever happens, don't rub. You can tear your face to pieces that way."

The hot water was not very hot, but Andy drank some and lay down on the bough mattress to plan his next moves. He remembered Morton, presumably still in the aircraft, but he had too much else on his mind to worry about him. He put his head on his outstretched arms and tried to imagine that he was warm.

In a few minutes he got up and went back to the job. A surprising amount had been done despite the incessant, whipping wind which made every step a moment of misery. More snow was piled against the back of the windbreak, which had grown half of another tier. It was now chest-high, and the men working on the inside were receiving a small amount of protection from it. In the center one man was down on his knees trying to clear a spot for a fireplace. Andy dropped beside him and said, "Wait a minute."

Within the eight-foot circle formed by the windbreak he marked a half dozen small spots and then began to clear one away. "We won't build one big fire," he said. "Several small ones are much more efficient and much warmer. You'll see."

After five minutes' work he had the first spot prepared. Without being asked John had brought a supply of the firewood which had been gathered and began to pull out the inside bark as he had seen Andy do. When he had enough of it, he went to the paratent for the candle and matches.

Andy took the bark pieces, shredded them, and built a tiny pyramid. Then someone said, "I've got a lighter."

"Let's have it," Andy answered. He placed the candle in the snow behind the windbreak, pulled off his gauntlets, and carefully lit the candle. When he had it going well, he used it to light the little pile of tinder.

"That's a neat trick," Preston Williams said.

"It saves matches," John explained, "and it gives you a lot longer time to get your fire going."

When the little blaze had fairly caught, Andy turned to

82

John. "You tend this one," he directed. "I'll get some others built."

"I can do that," Sam Welles volunteered. "You have more important things to look after." As he spoke, another cowlful of loose snow was pushed out of the tunnel. Two of the men picked it up, carried it around the end opening, and emptied it against the outer side of the windbreak. Then a digger appeared from the mouth of the snow cave. "I'm getting wet," he said, "and you warned about that."

Andy sent him to the paratent, which was still the best shelter available, and crawled inside the cave to inspect the work. Once in the tunnel, the bite of the wind was gone, and it seemed much warmer. The entranceway was now smooth and well packed on the bottom, but the opening at the end, where the main room would be, was still discouragingly small. Jim Hill was inside, working steadily with the little spade. "How does it look?" he asked.

"It's coming," Andy answered. "It's going to be dome-shaped, so that as the snow melts it will run down the walls and not drip in the middle of the floor."

"Good point," the copilot answered. "I don't mind working in here; at least it's out of that awful wind. And I see the point about the engine cowl. When we were getting it off I was pretty cold and I didn't thank you for the job. Now I do."

Andy answered by taking the spade and digging into the snow, which was well packed but not frozen solid. He cut it out in cubes and let Jim load them onto an empty cowl. It was quickly filled and was pushed outside to be emptied. Andy worked on for another ten minutes, and when he had finished, he was able to stand upright inside. "It will be easier from here on in," he said. "At least two men can work at digging, and that piece of metal you sent over will make a good cutter as soon as we finish with it outside."

Andy crawled back out, pushing a filled cowl section with him as he went. When he emerged, three of the small fires were going, and John was busily tending them all. "Don't let them get too big," Andy warned. "We don't have too much fuel, and we can't afford to waste any."

A particularly vicious gust of wind seized hold of them all and one of the small fires blew out. John relighted it with a brand from another and watched while the fourth little pyramid was being built.

Sam Welles, one of the newsmen, appeared lugging something in his hands. "Here's the food package from one of the life rafts," he announced. "It's darned heavy and I'm glad of it!" He dropped it on the packed area behind the windbreak and looked at Andy.

To the hungry, laboring men it was an electric moment. Work stopped as the announcement of food reminded each man of his gnawing hunger. Andy understood completely and took immediate action.

"I'll thaw out the rations right away," he said, "and we'll take turns eating as fast as I can get the food ready. But don't stop the digging. We have a long way to go yet, and if we aren't through in a few more hours, then it will be too late for the cave to do us any good."

7 The Snow Cave

Despite the severe cold, Andy removed his gauntlets and attacked the ninety-pound package of survival rations and gear which had been part of the twenty-man life-raft kit.

"How much food is there?" one of the men asked, a little anxiously.

"Enough to feed twenty men for three days. Two rafts should last us for six days at least, and probably for eight or nine days," Andy answered. He broke open the outer coverings and pulled out the first of the food packages. To the watching men it seemed disappointingly small. Andy placed it close to one of the small fires and then did the same with another.

"You probably wonder what's in there," he said, turning his

85

back to the unrelenting wind. "There are cereal bars, cheese bars, and pound cake. They'll all taste greasy, but be glad of it; they all have a lot of fat in them to generate heat in your body. Eat them slowly."

"Any cigarettes?" another man asked.

Andy shook his head. "No cigarettes. This is strictly survival material. But there is powdered milk, coffee, and tea, so we can keep the hot beverages coming. There are even some pans to melt the snow."

"How come you know all about it?" the timid reporter asked.

"Survival school," Andy answered. "Dad saw to it that I took all of the courses because we're out in the open a lot."

"Remind me to buy your father a steak dinner," Bernstein said, "as soon as we're back at Fort Richardson."

They were interrupted by another cowlful of snow being pushed out of the tunnel. A change of shift took place and John went in to take over the digging. Preston Williams went with him to help.

Andy brought out the melting pans and packed them with fresh, clean snow. "If any of you fellows do this," he cautioned, "be sure to pack the snow in tightly. If you don't, you'll burn out the bottom of the pan, and we can't afford to lose any."

Now that food was available in reasonable quantity, and was being warmed for immediate consumption, the frozen, hungry, tired men took new hope. At Andy's request two of them went for stones to surround the little fireplaces. By now five of the small fires were burning, and collectively they gave off a ring of heat which was a real blessing. The men took turns standing in the middle to let a little of the life-giving heat take some of the chill out of their bodies.

The windbreak continued to go up. Already its effect was considerable and behind its protection the chill factor was much reduced. It was possible to talk in near-normal tones, and the steady flicker of the little fires gave them all hope as well as warmth.

Soon the first of the food was passed out. Six of the men took time to eat, doing so slowly because the survival rations were, as Andy described them, chosen for fat content rather than tastiness. When the six had finished they relieved the men who were at work digging and piling up snow blocks around the entrance.

Andy and John ate with the second group. Although he had tried to push the thought out of his mind, Andy was very hungry, and he had been exerting himself heavily since the early morning. With the powdered tea he brewed a hot beverage for everyone, and the men responded wonderfully to its stimulating warmth. They went back to work with a will, and the filled cowls began to come out of the tunnel almost as fast as they could be hauled away and dumped. The outside of the windbreak was now firmly packed, and any danger of the wind's blowing it over was past.

Although the sun was not visible in the cloudy, storm-filled sky, Andy realized that the brief daylight would soon be over. "I'm going to abandon the fire over at the tent," he advised, "so we can let it go out. We're going to need a lot of firewood over here to warm the cave, and poles to build some of the things we're going to need. The windbreak is high enough; as soon as the storm lets up, I'll rig a parachute cover over it to make it both a tent and a signal for the rescue planes."

Captain Gregory had something to say. "Andy, the inside of the snow cave is beginning to look pretty good. When we caught on to how to dig, it went a lot faster. I'd guess we're three-quarters through."

Andy dropped to his knees, waited until a full cowling of

snow was pushed out, and then crawled in. After ten feet he went up the short ramp he had ordered and then stood up inside the drift. He was now in a fair-sized room. It was a good fifteen feet in diameter, as he had specified, with about a quarter section left to be excavated. The roof had been well cut into a rough dome shape and seemed to be firm and solid.

"Burrowing into this snowbank was a stroke of genius, Andy," the captain said. "When I first looked at it, I had no idea it could be used for a shelter. If anything, it seemed to make matters worse."

"There's no genius to it, sir," Andy answered. "I never made a snow cave before, but I knew about them. There are several different kinds, depending on how many people have to be protected and for how long. They're a lot of work to make, but well worth it."

"I just hope the roof doesn't cave in. If that happens, I think it would lick us all."

"As long as it's a good foot thick, we're all right," Andy answered. "We've got a lot more than that, I'm sure. That reminds me, we've got to have a vent hole and I'd better get started on it—there can't be much light left."

From the firewood that had been gathered Andy selected a piece of a small tree trunk, which was now a tapered pole about eight feet long. He stuck it upright in the snow and then went to the paratent to retrieve his survival kit. He took a ball of stout twine from the kit and with his knife cut off two pieces several feet in length. Next he gathered together two flat little piles of pine boughs, which he selected with some care. Satisfied, he passed the pieces of twine under them and then tied each of them carefully to one of his mukluks. When he had finished, he had an acceptable pair of improvised snowshoes.

Walking was awkward and difficult, but he did not have far

to go. He recovered the pole and then began a careful climb up one side of the big snowdrift. It was more than ten minutes' work to get to the top, where the wind caught him with its full fury. Andy leaned well into it and made a careful eye measurement of the top of the drift and the location of the entrance to the tunnel, which was now well below him. When he was satisfied that he had the location of the central room of the cave well spotted, he walked carefully over the snow with the aid of his improvised snowshoes and noted that it was firm and solid underfoot. That was good. He raised his pole, big end upward, into a vertical position and then pushed it down, at a deliberate slant, into the snow. It went a short distance and then stopped. Turning it like a drill, Andy forced it down into the drift until only a short length remained in sight. Then he felt it break through into the room below.

He heard a muffled shout and knew that the vent he was opening would be in good position. He pulled the pole up again and then widened the upper opening with his hands. When this was done, he built a snow dike on the windward side of the hole to prevent drifting snow from quickly plugging it up again. He would have liked to have had a ski pole to put upside down into the upper end as a snow guard, but nothing like that was available. If it gave any trouble, some sort of ducting could be removed from the airplane in the morning and used as a chimney.

His work completed, Andy slid down the far side of the drift and stuck his pole conveniently in the snow for future use if needed. He checked the condition of the little ring of fires and found them being well cared for by John, who appeared to be quite comfortable. Considerable heat was reflected back from the snow-block wall, and the space in the middle of the little fires was noticeably warm and comfortable.

"I think you've got it made," John said enthusiastically. Despite the glowering sky overhead, he was in a cheerful mood. He had eaten, he was comfortably warm, and a strong sense of adventure had replaced his former acute discomfort.

"At the moment it's not bad," Andy answered him, "but we have a long way to go yet before we're out of this. I've never heard of a snow cave collapsing, but it could happen. In that case, I wouldn't know what to do. I don't think we could all get out of it alive."

Another cowling full of snow appeared from the tunnel, and the reporter who had been pushing it stood up and looked at the sky. "Getting darker," he said. "But I don't mind now. We've got the cave finished."

Without replying anything, Andy crawled through the tunnel and then stood up inside the snow room. It was dark inside; what little light there was came in through the tunnel, and it was fading out rapidly. All of the men were assembled inside except for Jim Hill and his partner, who were out cutting firewood.

"The big job is over," Andy said. "We have plenty of roof over us, and we can be pretty comfortable here for a couple of weeks if we have to."

"At least it's inside out of the wind," one of the reporters said.

"Yes, it is," Andy agreed. "I'd like to tell you that we're all through, but it isn't so. We can sleep in here tonight the way it is and finish up in the morning, or, if you feel up to it, we can do the rest tonight and then be a lot more comfortable."

"Since we all had something to eat, and since your young friend out there with the fires is keeping the coffee coming," Sam Welles said, "I, for one, am in favor of finishing whatever remains to be done."

"Me too," Bernstein added. "What's next, chief?"

Andy flushed a little, despite the cold. "Forget the chief part," he said. "We need to cut six sleeping rooms off this main cave. That isn't as bad as it sounds. They're only five feet square and six feet deep—you cut them like the spokes of a wheel. Then we need one room a little larger for a latrine; that's important."

Captain Gregory nodded his agreement. "I was wondering about that," he said.

"If we still feel like it, the final thing would be to cut a little storage space for our supplies. I'll build a fireplace and get some heat going in here."

"It's hard to realize that we're inside a snowdrift," Williams remarked.

"Think about all the shoveling you've been doing, Preston, and you'll get the message," Welles said, and there was a little ripple of laughter.

"What are we waiting for?" one of the men remarked. "We ought to be able to cut out those sleeping holes pretty fast if we get to it."

As work began once more, Andy crawled outside to discover that the darkness had almost come. Fighting the wind which seemed stronger after he had been out of it for a few minutes, he worked his way back to the paratent, which was still standing, and retrieved the fire reflector. He also gathered up the poles which had formed the bed frame and with this load returned to the snow cave. John had guessed what he was doing, and met him halfway. "Anything else?" he asked.

"The cooking dish," Andy answered, "and as many of the boughs from the mattress as you can handle without too much trouble."

John brought them all; when he reached the mouth of the

cave he knew that Andy wanted to have them brought inside. Although the men were tired, the comparative comfort of the cave and the continuing supply of hot coffee and tea kept them going without complaint. One of the sleeping niches had already been dug out and a second was well under way. By the time John arrived, Andy had the fire reflector lying flat in the middle of the floor and was covering it with stones. When he had finished, he took the boughs John had brought and spread them out, all facing one way, in the completed sleeping alcove. "That's how to do it," he said. "It makes a good mattress and keeps you off the cold snow. There are lots of boughs outside. Pick your own roommates and whatever sleeping room you want. Whoever is the most tired can have this one."

"No, that's yours," the captain said. "You've certainly earned it. Since we may not get all of the sleeping rooms done tonight, how do you want the latrine dug? We ought to do that next."

With a stick Andy sketched on the snow floor. "A little bigger room, that's all. It's best if you can put a little offset in the entrance. When we're through with the shovel, it can be left in there. Then whoever uses the latrine can throw on a little snow to make it sanitary for the next one, and so on."

"Right," the captain said. With the edge of the spade he traced the dimensions on the face of the snow wall and then cut in. Half an hour later the latrine room was ready, and with the aid of the sheet of metal, another sleeping room had also been prepared. As soon as it was ready and the snow was hauled away, more boughs were brought in and another mattress quickly laid.

Andy had been busy with his inside fire. He located it carefully in relationship to the overhead vent he had drilled and soon had it going. It was a small, controlled blaze, but it immediately lit up the interior and gave it a sense of warmth and security. Then he went outside and retrieved the rest of the survival package from the life raft. When he had it beside the fire, he began to thaw out some more of the rations and set one of the water heaters he had been using outside on the warming stones.

By the cheering light of the fire, two more sleeping niches were carved out of the snow in much better time, and the excess snow was pushed outside. "Two more and we're done," someone remarked. "One more bedroom and the supply room. That ought to be the easiest of the lot."

"We're getting the hang of it now," Jim Hill commented. "If I had realized how much work we had ahead of us this morning, I don't think I would have had the courage to attempt it. Now that we're almost through, I'm mighty glad we did."

"Amen," commented the timid reporter, who didn't seem so timid any more.

"I just realized something," Sam Welles said. "There's only ten of us, and two to a room means five rooms. We made six, or are making six. Isn't that what you called for?" He looked at Andy, who nodded gravely.

One of the men, who had been digging, put down the little spade and turned toward the others. "I want to say something," he announced, "it's been on my mind for some time."

"Go ahead, Chick," Preston Williams invited.

"It's about Morton, of course. I've been fighting with my conscience on this one and I want you to know what I think."

He stopped and gathered his breath. "This is the first time in more than twenty years that I have done any hard manual labor. My doctor has advised me strongly against it, but that's another matter—we have all been in a near-desperate situation and everyone has had to do his part to get us out of it."

There was almost total silence inside the snow cave. The fire crackled softly, but the sound of the still unyielding wind outside was muffled by the entrance tunnel and the thickness of the snow that surrounded them all.

"I hope," the speaker went on, "that I'm as decent and humanitarian as the next man. If any one of us couldn't do his part, I'd gladly add to my own efforts to help him out. But Morton is another matter. Of all of us he is probably the best physical specimen, and if he had been here working beside us, things would have been considerably easier."

"He wouldn't," someone remarked.

"I know it," the man called Chick went on. "When he had a slight advantage, with a little food, he pushed it for all he was worth. When he bragged how smart he was, I wanted to go outside and vomit. Now"—he paused for effect—"I know what's going to happen. Anytime from now on Morton is going to come crawling through that entrance we all worked so hard to dig, and he's going to open that big mouth of his and say something like, 'Hello, suckers!' Then he'll warm himself in front of our fire and make himself comfortable in this place we all nearly killed ourselves to make. And he'll probably sneer at the young man over there who, as far as I am concerned, is the one who's saved all our necks so far."

"I agree completely with that last part," Captain Gregory interrupted, "but I have to add something. Morton revolts me as much as he does any of you, perhaps even more so because he interfered when I was trying to meet an emergency situation according to my responsibility. But, speaking of responsibility, he is one of my passengers and I just can't abandon him because he's done everything possible to make himself an unwanted member of our company."

"That's right," Chick acknowledged. "You have to look after him, I'll concede that. If you didn't, the rest of us would,

94

on the basis that he is, at least technically, a human being and none of us would be willing just to let him die. But, as worn out as I am tonight, I just won't dig out his bed for him and fix it up with a nice bough mattress. He can come in, he can drink our hot coffee, and, if necessary, he can have part of our food, *but he makes his own bed.*"

There was a quick murmur of agreement.

"It will give me the greatest pleasure to sit here and watch him do it," Isaac Bernstein added. "And he isn't going to pile up his loose snow in the middle of the room, either."

"He won't do that," Captain Gregory said grimly. "He'll remove his own snow and then, as far as I'm concerned, he's on the firewood detail until further notice."

Preston Williams looked toward Andy. "Apart from Mr. Morton's bunk, which I suspect no one will be too anxious to share with him, is there anything else we need to prepare?"

Andy stood up. "There's one more easy thing," he said. "Where is the life raft?"

"About a hundred feet outside the entrance," Jim Hill answered.

"Well, if somebody wants to give me a hand rolling it inside here, we can all be a lot more comfortable."

Two men immediately got up. One of them was the timid reporter, Boyd. "We'll do that," he said. "It should be easy enough. It's on the cabin door, and that's a good sled."

Bernstein got up. "Many hands make light work. I'll come too."

"And me," Captain Gregory added. The four men crawled out. In less than ten minutes they were back, pushing the rolled-up life raft ahead of them. Andy opened it up and with Bernstein's help began to lay it out.

"I'd appreciate it," he said, "if everybody would take hold

of this around the rim. I can't spread it all of the way out because of the fire, but if you lift it well up, then I'll be able to inflate it. Without the ration pack it isn't too heavy."

The men quickly formed a circle and held the limp raft, fully extended, three or four feet above the snow floor. With his knife Andy cut a five-foot circle out of the center, which allowed clearance for the fire. Then he pulled the inflating bottle. With a strong hissing sound, which was magnified by the close confines of the chamber, the raft filled out until it was almost the size of the room itself.

"O.K., put it down," Andy directed.

When the inflated raft was eased down into position, it covered all but the center of the snow pack; the heavy inflated rubber ring around its outside edge reached up to the bottom of the sleeping alcoves.

"All right," Andy said. "This gives us plenty of comfortable sitting space. That's one of the purposes of the big outer ring. The floor of the raft will keep our feet warm, and if anybody wants to lie down beside the fire, he can do it without getting wet."

"This is really something," Boyd said. "We not only have a comfortable cave, but it's furnished as well."

"And darned lucky that the raft just fits," another man commented.

"Lucky my foot," Preston Williams interjected. "About four hours ago our young leader here told us exactly how big to make this cave, and how high off the floor to cut the sleeping ledges." He turned toward Andy. "You were figuring on the size of this raft all along, weren't you?"

Andy's face looked tired by the flickering light of the fire. "In any survival situation," he said, "you try to improvise as much as you can and make use of what you have. That's the lesson we were all taught."

"Are we all through?" Chick asked.

"All of the construction work is done," Andy answered. "Tomorrow, if things aren't any better, we'll want to improve the roof vent with some kind of duct from the airplane. Otherwise we're about as well off as we can expect. I'd guess that it's twenty below ouside. In here, it's at least forty above, and that's pretty warm for this country. Besides, we're out of the wind, and that's the most important thing. The chill factor in here is only a fraction of what it is outside."

Captain Gregory stood up. "I have a job to do. I'll probably need some help, so, Jim, will you come along? Remember, gentlemen, that our Mr. Morton is going to be pretty cold by now and he may be a different person. I should have gone for him sooner. He didn't do any of the work, but with his frozen food and without our hot coffee, I'd say he's been paying the price."

"All right, bring him in," one of the men said wearily.

The words were hardly out of his mouth when there was a noise of some uncertain kind outside. Automatically a quick, complete hush fell, and everyone strained to listen.

Outside, someone was singing.

It was not a normal singing, but a wild, distorted sound which seemed to echo in a weird, lonesome world of its own. There was no recognizable melody, nothing that could be called a tune.

As Captain Gregory started toward the tunnel entrance, Preston Williams raised his hand and said quietly, "Wait."

The singing became louder. There was no mistaking Morton's loud, harsh tones. In a few moments he could be heard right outside, and it was clear he had found the entrance to the cave.

"I'm glad," Jim Hill said, "I was afraid we might have waited too long."

"Where would we have put him?" Williams asked. "Anyhow, he's coming in."

Everyone sat quietly while Morton could be heard making his way through the short tunnel. No one got up to help him. Then he appeared.

He was an incredible sight. His face was an allover gray with white spots the size of silver dollars in several places. His eyebrows were hidden behind frost. His parka hood was pulled down around his throat, leaving his head bare. It appeared to be covered with ice. As he crawled he clutched a bottle in one thick gauntlet and had his remaining box lunch in the other.

When he was clear of the tunnel he tried to rise to his feet, but he was almost unable to keep his balance.

"Drunk as a hoot owl!" Boyd said.

Morton tried to look at the fire, but his eyes would not come to focus. He attempted one step forward, and fell heavily across the inflated ring of the life raft. Then he lay still.

Andy got up quickly and pulled off his gloves. Taking Morton's arms he pulled him onto the flat floor of the life raft and then bent down over him. Morton was now clearly unconscious and his cheeks were strangely distended. Carefully Andy pulled his jaw open so that his lips were well parted. A solid chunk of ice fell from between his teeth and dropped onto the orange rubber floor of the inflated life raft.

Andy looked up quickly at Captain Gregory. "He's in bad shape," he reported. "He's seriously frostbitten, almost his whole face is frozen. He's been trying to eat snow, and on top of it he's drunk a lot of alcohol."

The pilot dropped down onto one knee beside the now silent Morton. After a closer look he turned towards the others. "Has anyone here had any medical experience? Any at all?"

There was no answer.

"Andy, I guess it's up to you," Gregory said. "Can you help him?"

Andy shook his head. "I'll try my very best," he said, "but I don't know how much I can do. After what he's done to himself, it's going to be pretty much touch and go. Start heating some water right away."

8 Morton

There was a general quiet in the snow cave as Morton's condition became clear to everyone. Captain Gregory was inclined to blame himself for not having brought the big man in sooner, but several others were quick to point out that the cave had actually been habitable for only a few minutes when Morton arrived. Before that, there was no place where he could have been taken except the paratent, and that offered inadequate shelter for a man in such serious condition.

With Bernstein's help Andy removed the frozen man's parka, and folding it, used one corner as a pillow for his head. He was completely unconscious, breathing with great heavy surges of his chest with clear pauses between his gasps for air. His

breath was foul and the stubble on his chin flecked with ice crystals.

"What I really need is some hot towels," Andy said. "Has anybody got anything I can use?"

"I have," Preston Williams answered. "I carry towels in my luggage, and my suitcase is on top of the pile in the cabin. I'll go and get it."

"Do you feel up to it?" Andy asked.

"Oh, certainly. I'm warm now, and I've had lots of good hot coffee. No trouble at all." He pulled up his parka hood and pushed his hands into his arctic gauntlets.

"I'll come with you if you like," Jim Hill offered. "I don't think one man should go out there alone. The weather is fierce and you might lose your way."

Captain Gregory nodded his approval. "Look around while you're there, Jim, and see if you see anything else we might need. The Very pistol, for one thing; we might have to shoot a flare."

"There are flares in the life-raft kit," Andy said, "day and night types. But if you see anything else that looks useful, bring it along."

The two men departed. Trying to be helpful, John picked up Morton's frozen box lunch, which was like a solid chunk of ice, and started to put it near the fire to thaw it out. "Look," he said, "here's a funny thing. It's black all over the bottom."

Bernstein took it and examined the discolored area. "I think I can explain it," he said. "It's smoke and char. Morton must have tried to thaw it out with matches and didn't succeed."

"He must have used a lot of matches," John commented. "That was a foolish thing to do. Andy told me that in the open, matches are a critical item."

"It seems to me," Boyd said, "that Morton made every mistake in the book. I hate to see him in the shape he's in, but he brought it on himself. I want to apologize to everyone for even thinking of voting for him. I guess I was hungry and the idea of part of a sandwich was too strong."

"Don't worry about it," Bernstein answered him. "In a way he made a good case for himself. He simply didn't know the first thing about what to do. Of course none of us did, really, except Andy."

"I won't dispute that a bit," Captain Gregory said. "He has the knowledge, and he knows how to put it to use. And he's done a man's work, there's no doubt of that. I know my congressman well, and when we're all safely back, I'm going to suggest to him that Andy be nominated for the Air Force Academy."

Andy stopped what he was doing and looked up. "If you mean that, sir, could you make it West Point? Dad's an Army man, you know."

From the life-raft kit John extracted one of the folding buckets and poured in all the hot water that was available. Setting the bucket as close to the fire as he dared, he packed fresh snow into the melting pans and put them back over the flame.

With a handkerchief, which was inadequate for the job, Andy began to apply hot water to the top of Morton's head. Carefully he washed away the accumulation of ice crystals from the correspondent's thinning hair which had been, in part, protected by his parka hood.

"How about giving him something hot to drink?" Chick proposed. "I know better than to suggest any more alcohol, but some coffee to thaw him out might be a good idea."

"As soon as he's conscious I will," Andy answered. "It's dangerous to try to give any fluids to an unconscious person. They're always doing it in the movies, but it's wrong. For one thing, the person can't swallow, and the stuff could just as easily go down his windpipe into his lungs."

"Can't we revive him?" Boyd asked.

"If he stays unconscious a little while, it will spare him a lot of pain," Andy said. "When his face starts thawing out, it will be pretty rough, and he's not the kind of guy who'll be able to sit quietly and take it. He'll want to rub, and if he does, then he may tear his skin away."

It was quiet while Andy, with his handkerchief, applied warm water to the worst parts of Morton's face. He was still patiently working at it when Preston Williams crawled back in, followed by Jim Hill.

"You should see the plane," the copilot said. "Everything's torn to pieces. When Morton was looking for something he could eat or wear to keep warm, he must have emptied out all the luggage on the floor. And get this—there's a pile of about forty burned-out matches near his seat."

Williams handed over two towels which he had tucked into his parka. "I don't blame the man for not respecting private property, considering the position he was in, but he certainly wrecked everything in sight."

"He would have made a great leader," Chick commented.

"Fast talk and true leadership are two different things," Williams replied. Then he watched as Andy soaked one of the towels in the bucket of warm water, wrung it out, and applied it to Morton's face much as a barber does while shaving a customer. Only the tip of the man's nose remained uncovered.

"I'm going to need lots of hot water, hotter than this," Andy said. "John, get as much ready as you can and try to keep what's in the pail as warm as possible."

"I'll help," Chick volunteered.

"I thought you couldn't stand the sight of Morton," someone said.

"I can't," Chick replied. "But I want to see Andy here get the credit for bringing us *all* back alive. Let's leave it at that."

While Chick heated up the two towels alternately in the warm water, Andy kept applying them to Morton's still frozen face. Once the big man stirred and appeared to be trying to say something, then he lapsed back into unconsciousness. John took one of the pans off the fire and poured steaming water into the pail. As a result the next towel was much hotter, and Andy nodded his approval.

"I want to get him thawed out as fast as I can," he said. "It's the right way to do it, and the more we can get accomplished while he's out, the better."

"Is he likely to be a problem when he comes to?" Williams asked.

"I think so," Andy answered without stopping his work. "He's drunk, for one thing, and his face will hurt him terribly. He'll want to dig at it, and we can't let him."

"Then maybe we'd better figure out some method of restraint while we have a chance," the captain suggested. "He's a brawny guy and won't be easy to hold. In his condition we won't be able to reason with him, either."

"I think I know how to do that," Chick said. "We can fold his arms and then tie them with something across his back. That won't hurt him, but it will keep him from harming himself."

"Good idea," Gregory said. "Sit him up for a moment and we'll do it." With the aid of an extra sweater which one of the men provided, Morton was trussed up. The sleeves were pulled down over his hands and then tied at the bottoms, his arms were crossed, and then some of Andy's twine was used to tie them together, with the line running behind his back. Then he was laid down again and Andy continued to apply the hot towels.

Presently they began to see results. The sharp white spots softened, and the gray color faded to a more normal tone. Once more the big man on the floor turned and moaned, but he remained unconscious. Andy worked rapidly, changing the towels as soon as one became even slightly cool. Each time he uncovered Morton's face he looked at it carefully and studied the pattern of the disappearing mottled spots. "I think he might make it," he said finally. "But he'll have to stay out of the arctic for a long while, because flesh once frostbitten is more susceptible the next time."

"I think he's coming around," Captain Gregory noted. As he spoke, Morton clearly made an effort to raise his head and look about him. Andy lifted off the towel so that he could see.

"Whasamatter with my arms?" Morton said, coming out of the fog which had surrounded him. Bernstein, who was behind him, helped him to sit up. "My face," Morton yelled. "Whatcha done to my face?" He began to cry.

"Prop him up against the side of the raft," Andy directed. Bernstein and Chick pulled the big man over and placed him so that he would be reasonably comfortable. "My face!" Morton screamed, and his voice cut like a volley of sharp knives through the inside of the stark-white cave.

Gregory stood in front of him. "Can you hear me?" he asked.

In agony Morton looked up at him. "I hear ya," he said heavily.

"All right, then listen carefully. Your face was frozen, get that, frozen just like a cake of ice."

Morton continued to cry, sobbing like a small child. Tears rolled out of the corners of his eyes.

"Your face has been thawed out," the pilot continued. "Andy did it. Do you know who Andy is?"

Morton appeared to lose again some of his consciousness. When he spoke he mumbled so his words were barely understandable. "Andy, he's tha' fresh kid ... tried t' tell me I was wrong—*me*. Hate tha' fresh kid..."

"If your face weren't so sore, I'd slap it to bring you around," Gregory said, biting off his words in a controlled fury. "That boy Andy probably saved your life; in fact I'm sure of it, and if you get out of this with any skin left on your face, you'll have him to thank."

Morton's body seemed to relax, and the shadow of a whole new mood passed across his raw face. "Ya mean he did something for me?"

"You bet he did, he did something for all of us. If it weren't for him, you'd be lying out there right now, face down and dying in the snow. Can you understand that?"

Morton began to blubber. "Thanks, Andy," he said thickly.

"He needs more towels," Andy interrupted. "Another ten minutes anyway. He isn't going to like it, but it's got to be done."

Despite Morton's half-articulate protests, and his sobs of pain when the hot towels were applied, Andy continued with the work until he peeled off one last towel, inspected the heavy man's face, and declared himself satisfied.

"The next thing is to get some hot soup and some food into him," he declared.

"Some coffee might sober him up better," Chick suggested.

"He'll sober up," Andy said. "I think the soup will do him more good. How are the cubes holding out?"

"We have seven left," John replied. "Six in a minute." He unwrapped one and dropped it into a pan of warming water.

Morton's face had begun to get back some color, but there were angry red and blue spots on it where the blood was trying to force its way through the tiny veins which had been frozen tightly shut. John checked the condition of his box lunch and found that it was slowly thawing out. There was a carton of milk inside and a can of tomato juice, but they were still like pieces of ice. A piece of fried chicken in a wax-paper bag was still inedible. The two sandwiches appeared to be ready.

As soon as the cube was dissolved, John poured out a cupful of the hot soup. With a spoon which had been in the life-raft kit, he began to feed it, a little at a time, to Morton. The big

107

man, who was now considerably deflated, sucked it off the spoon with a loud noise. When Andy felt that he had had enough this way, he nodded to put the cup up to Morton's lips.

When he had finished, the now beaten man relaxed back against the inflated rim of the raft and seemed to find his senses once more. "You can untie me, boys," he said. "I'm not going to hurt anybody."

"We're not worried about that," Gregory answered him. "While you weren't yourself we didn't want to risk letting you rub your face. If you did that, you could have torn the skin right off. It's still very tender."

"You're telling me!" Morton said. "If that's all that's worrying you, I'll take the responsibility. Untie me and I promise before witnesses not to go near my face with my hands. Can you trust me to keep my word?"

"If you don't, it will be you who suffer, not we," Gregory replied. "O.K., untie him."

Bernstein heaved himself wearily to his feet. "Since Gill is in no condition to help himself," he announced, "I'll cut out his sleeping ledge for him."

"Let him sleep by the fire," Andy suggested. "You've done more than enough for one day. He'll be comfortable there."

"We'll have to set up a schedule of watches," Captain Gregory said. "That will be Jim's and my job. I'll take the first trick."

"No," Boyd answered. "There are eleven of us, and we can all take a turn."

"Let me be first," John proposed, "I'll keep the fire going and some coffee warm for whoever wants it. I think we have enough firewood to last until morning."

Quickly it was decided who would relieve John and what the rotation would be during the night. Jim offered to plug up the entrance tunnel with the cabin door from the airplane, but Andy vetoed it, saying that the ventilation was needed, particularly with a fire going. After that there was no more discussion. The bone-weary men lay down, two to each bough mattress, and within ten minutes they were all asleep. John sat, alone with his thoughts, beside the small fire. He looked up and saw a drop of water running down the inside of the snow wall; eventually it froze into a tiny globule of ice and remained in position halfway from roof to floor.

He was not cold any more. Knowing there was plenty, he helped himself to a cup of warm soup and felt that no matter what happened now, he would not worry any more. Andy had brought them all this far, and he had complete confidence that his friend would somehow see them all the way through. He listened to the crackling of the little fire and the heavy breathing of Morton, who lay still and asleep a few feet away. When the burly reporter woke in the morning, he might have sense enough to realize what had been done for him.

John had wanted very much to see the arctic; he had counted the days until it would be time to leave California for Alaska. Now he was seeing the arctic with a vengeance. Even more, to just a small extent, he was beginning to understand it.

At that exact time an urgent meeting was being held in the Rescue Coordination Center at Elmendorf Air Force Base, Anchorage, Alaska. A weather officer was talking to the rescue specialists and the others who were assembled there.

"The pattern of the storm is this," he said, pointing to a map which had just been drawn. "The main body of the frontal system has now moved east and will have cleared the area of maximum probability by early morning. Wind conditions will then be westerly at twenty to twenty-five knots. Unfortunately, this will be accompanied by a further drop in temperature."

"How about the chill factor?" the vice-commander asked.

"Not good, sir," the weather officer, who was a captain, continued. "The lessening of the wind is a great help, of course, but the lower temperature indicates that we should get the survivors out as quickly as possible. It may get as cold as forty below."

Most of the men in the room unconsciously looked at Colonel Driscoll, who was present but who so far had taken no part in the discussion. His boy was out there somewhere on the snow, and they all knew it. The strain was even greater because his wife was vacationing in Florida and she had not been told.

Colonel Walton, the Air Force vice-commander, called on the next man he wanted to hear. He turned to Major Towers, the chief medical expert on cold-weather survival. "If Colonel Driscoll will forgive me," he said, "I would like to have a realistic picture of just what their chances are."

The medical officer hesitated several seconds before replying. "I don't like to say this in Colonel Driscoll's presence," he answered, "but I'm forced to conclude that they are not good. This is the second night they will be out in the open. As yet, all that we know for a definite fact is that they are down, somewhere out in harsh country. Since there has been no radio communication of any kind, we have to assume there was a crash; of course atmospherics may have prevented any weak signals from being heard."

"Just how competent was the pilot?" the vice-commander asked.

An operations officer answered that one. "Very competent, sir. He's a man of long experience, an Air Force reservist with the rank of major and an instructor pilot. The only bad thing I can see is the fact that this was his first trip into the arctic.

Neither he nor his copilot has had any cold-weather experience."

"They have now," Colonel Walton commented grimly. "How about the others?"

"We've checked all of their backgrounds, sir, and unfortunately none of the men has had any extended experience up here. It's definite that none of them has been to cold-weather survival school."

"Andy has," Colonel Driscoll said, speaking for the first time.

"Yes, sir, that's right. Of all of the people on the flight he was far and away the best-informed on survival procedures. Assuming that he came through the crash all right, and I'd like very much to make that assumption, then he would be an invaluable member of the party."

Colonel Walton turned to Andy's father. "I've heard about your boy," he said. "I understand that he's very resourceful. Do you have any comment that might help us?"

Despite the strain he was under, Colonel Driscoll answered promptly and carefully. "Andy *is* very resourceful, I think I can claim that for him. He's a good man in the open, and I don't hesitate to apply the word 'man,' because I'm confident he will more than hold up his end. If there is any way to bring the survivors through this, assuming that he is one of them and not too badly injured to be of use, my best guess is that he will pull it off. That is, if they'll listen to him. Because of his age, they may decide that he doesn't know what he's talking about. That would be a mistake."

"I know Bill Gregory pretty well," the operations officer said. "I knew him down in the south forty-eight, and my opinion is that if Andy is all right and has knowledge that Bill needs, he'll make use of it. Bill isn't one to overlook any good bets."

"It looks to me," Colonel Walton said, "as if Andy is the

best hope we have at the moment. All right, alert all available SAR [search and rescue] aircraft to be ready to go prior to daybreak. I want them over the most probable areas as soon as there's light enough to see things on the ground. Keep them at it until we have a positive location or until there's no more light with which to work. Maximum radar and radio coverage on all frequencies corresponding to radio equipment on the C-47."

"We'll handle everything, sir," the rescue officer said.

"Good. Colonel Driscoll, I'd like to invite you to be my guest here at rescue-control center. I'll have quarters assigned close by. I know what this means to you."

"If you have no objections, sir," Colonel Driscoll answered, "I'd like to go out with the search parties. Into the most probable area, if possible."

"Of course," the vice-commander agreed. He looked at the search chart and made a decision. "According to the last radar contact we had, they should be about here." He stopped and pointed. "Captain Meyers will be flying that sector; why don't you go with him?"

"I'll do that," Colonel Driscoll said. "Thank you very much."

It was a little before ten in the morning when the search plane, flying at five thousand feet, came over the place where the plane had crashed. Colonel Driscoll sat in the aircraft, nerves tense, anxiously looking out the window. He tried to study every bit of the snow-covered ground below. But the storm below had raged for two days, and its screaming winds had piled the snow high on every exposed object. Consequently, although he flew almost over it, he did not see the drift-covered airplane. The tracks in the snow and the air marker which Captain Gregory had begun to stamp out had long since been covered. The paratent had collapsed and its brightly colored parachute cover was shrouded in the everlastingly white blanket. The entrance to the snow cave was all but invisible. So the rescue plane flew on. On the chart which he was meticulously keeping on his lap, the navigator marked the location *Negative.*

9 *Icepick Seven*

When the sound of the plane penetrated into the snow cave, Jim Hill was the first man on his feet. He literally dived into the tunnel and made his way outside as fast as he could. The aircraft was overhead by the time he reached the snow windbreak. Although it was bitter cold and he did not have his parka on, he ran out into the open and waved his arms. And although he knew that it was an utterly hopeless thing to do, he shouted. He continued to jump up and down and to wave his arms until the plane was all but out of sight in the sky. By this time Captain Gregory was beside him and three of the others.

With mixed emotions Jim went back inside the snow cave

to don his parka. The rest remained outside in the hope that the aircraft might make another pass. Bernstein and Boyd tried frantically to assemble a pile of boughs in order to start a signal fire, but the depth of the snow and the fierce cold made the hasty attempt a failure. Discouraged, the men returned inside, where Captain Gregory held a quick council of war.

"They're looking for us, and they've got the right place," he announced. "It's only a question of time until they're overhead again. Jim and I will try to get the radios started in the aircraft. I don't hold much hope for success, but we'll do our best. As for whatever else we should do, I'm going to leave that to Andy. He's called every turn right so far, and I think he'll know best."

"Tell us what to do," Chick said.

"First of all, we need an air marker," Andy said. "We can make one on the snow. Since we don't need any supplies urgently, a big circle would be the best bet. We can tramp one out and then color it with the dye marker that we have in the life-raft kit. That should make it visible for a long way, and it won't take too long."

"That sounds like a three-man job to get it done quickly," Bernstein said. "I need two more." Two men were on their feet immediately; new hope had given them fresh energy.

"It's very cold out," Jim warned. "Bundle up well."

"How bright is it?" Andy asked.

"Very bright, I still can hardly see in here."

"Then we've got to have sunglasses," Andy declared. "Is anybody equipped?"

Two pairs of glasses were produced.

"That's not enough," Andy said. He took out his knife and picked up the carton which had held Morton's box lunch. He slit off a long strip of cardboard and began to cut it into shape.

In a minute or two he had a pair of cardboard glasses, but of course they had no lenses. In the place where the glass should have gone he cut two narrow slits in the cardboard and then tried them on. "These will work," he announced. "They aren't the best, but they'll do fine under arctic conditions."

The three men departed to make the marker.

"John and I have something to do," Andy told those who remained. "If the three of you feel up to it, we still need a signal fire. We may not get to light it, but if someone comes over at night, it might make the difference between being seen and being missed. And it's helpful by day, too, if it sends up a good column of smoke."

"Any special instructions?" Chick said.

"Just make a good pile of branches and leave a place where we can put some tinder inside. We'll light it, if we have to, with a brand from the inside fire. That will be the quickest way."

Morton struggled to his feet. "I'll help, too," he volunteered.

"Don't," Andy advised. "Your face isn't in condition to take any more cold. If you'll keep the fire going and the coffee hot, that would be a big help."

Closing his parka tightly, and seeing that John did the same, Andy led the way outside. He went directly to the pile of firewood and looked it over. Apparently it did not please him, so he took the little hand ax and made his way to the thin stand of small trees which was now much depleted by the cutting which had been done. He looked over what was available and then selected a small sapling which had been rejected because it offered little in the way of wood for either construction or burning. Andy cut it down and took off the few branches, then he trimmed down the remaining pole and stripped off what little bark there was.

116

Carrying it with him, he went to the spot, not far away, where the paratent had stood. In the now much lighter wind he recovered the piece of parachute silk and spread it out on the ground. From among the poles he had used in building the tent he selected a salvage piece about five feet long. Then, reaching into his parka, he produced one of the rolls of twine which had been part of his survival kit.

"Now what?" John asked.

By way of reply Andy laid the two sticks down on the silk and lashed them together in the form of a large cross. The main member was a good eight feet tall, while the crosspiece was about five. Then, with the twine, Andy tied the ends of the cross together so that the line formed a rough four-sided figure, with the wood pieces holding it at the corners.

"I began to get the idea," John said. "The parachute cloth is next, is that right?"

"It is," Andy answered. "You can give me a hand, now, if you want to."

With his knife he cut the cloth so that it was the same shape as the framework, with a good six inches left all around. Rummaging in the pockets of his parka, he came up with a large and ungainly-looking needle. "You can make a whole lot of things out of parachutes," he explained, "but for most of them you have to do some sewing. Or it makes it a lot easier. That's why I always carry this needle. You can make one if you have to, but it takes a lot of time." Then he set to work, using discarded shroud line as thread. With John holding the work for him, he rapidly sewed the parachute cloth to the frame he had made. It was not an elegant job, but it held together, and that was all that it was designed to do. When the job had been completed, John was looking at one of the biggest kites he had ever seen.

"Will it fly?" he asked.

"It ought to in this wind," Andy replied. "You might cut up some strips of the parachute to make a tail while I rig it."

While John did as he had been directed, Andy used more shroud line to make a proper bend in the kite and to provide a hitch to which the ground line could be attached. Then he tied on what remained of his twine, and the kite was ready.

"The line is too short," he said, "but I've got some more twine, and after we get it up, we can tie another piece onto the end. It will be easiest that way."

"Do you think anyone will be able to spot it?" John inquired. "I know it's bright-colored, but only if you see one face of it."

"That's a good point," Andy allowed, "but this kite they're going to see another way, if it works—thanks to a little something the British came up with during World War II called radar."

"Not off a cloth and wood kite," John pointed out. "It takes metal."

"Exactly. Do you want to go in and warm up, or would you like to try something with me?"

"I'm fine, as long as I keep my face out of the wind."

"Good, then how about getting that piece of engine cowling over by the door to the cave? It's the lighter half, I think."

While Andy carried the kite carefully, keeping its edge into the wind, John retrieved the piece of aluminum cowling. Knowing what Andy had in mind, he hefted it and realized that it was indeed quite light. The whole plan was now clear in his mind.

When he reached the open area, where the wind was still cutting despite its lessened force, he helped Andy to tie the

piece of cowling to a shroud line and then to the center of the kite itself.

It took three attempts to get the kite into the air. The first time it came nosing quickly down and would have smashed if it had not landed in deep snow. After more tail line was added, it was tried again, but it managed to slip sideways to the wind and came down once more. Each time Andy made patient adjustments until, on the third attempt, the kite bit into the wind and climbed, dangling the piece of cowling below it as though it weren't there.

When the short roll of twine had been played out, John held the kite against its strong pull while Andy tied on another section. Then, as the added line was played out, the kite rose until it was well up into the sky.

"I'll keep it up for a while," Andy said. "You go inside and warm up. Then come out and relieve me. After that we'll take turns, changing every fifteen minutes or so. You know how to fly a kite, don't you?"

Despite the cold, John grinned. "That's something we do down south," he answered. "Try me; I'll take over."

Andy handed over the line, and within a few seconds John had proved his point. Released from the kite duty, Andy plodded over and inspected the air marker, which was now complete. Then he made one more trek and had a look at the signaling bonfire that had been built. It lacked something in science, but it had been willingly done and was ready to fulfill its purpose. When he had finished his inspections, Andy turned to find two very cold pilots approaching him.

"We did our best with the radios," Captain Gregory said, "but the power supplies just wouldn't go. I'm sorry. What's the kite for?"

"Radar reflection," Jim Hill answered. "I saw them put it up. There's a piece of cowling under it. It's jumping all over the place, but somebody might just see it."

Sergeant Philip Biddle at the AC&W (Aircraft Control and Warning) station took a long look at the face of the tube before him and then picked up a phone. "I've got a funny bogie," he reported. "It appears airborne, but stationary." He repeated the coordinates according to the classified map before him. "It doesn't show up when the MTI [moving target indicator] is on. Do you read it?"

The radar operator at the next station switched his controls, directed the antenna to the proper quadrant, and had a look. "I show it too," he reported. Then he carefully read off the position as his station revealed it and the two were compared. As soon as this was done, Sergeant Biddle picked up another phone, which was of a different color, and instantly a light went on in a very secret room at Elmendorf. It was noted almost immediately, and the line was answered.

"Stationary bogie, confirmed," the sergeant reported, and gave the exact location. "Altitude under one thousand feet, but clearly airborne."

That was a new one, but the word was flashed at once to the NORAD control center at Colorado Springs, to the headquarters of SAC, and to the Pentagon. Since the target appeared stationary, it was duly noted, but the complex defense response system was not yet alerted. Within two minutes Elmendorf reported that a plane was down close to that exact location and that a search-and-rescue flight would be diverted to investigate. The target remained on scope, still stationary and apparently peaceful. NORAD kept track, but by decision of the duty commander an apparently all clear was sent out to the rest of the network. The alert crews waiting in their bunkers for a possible immediate call to duty at any hour of any day throughout the year were not ever aware that the AC&W line had turned up any form of an unexplained echo.

In the Rescue Coordination Center the officer in charge scanned the plotting board before him, picked up a microphone, and called for Icepick Seven.

Icepick Seven responded. She was a C-119 Flying Boxcar that belonged to the Air Force Reserve and was in Alaska, with a flight from March Air Force Base, Riverside, California, on a routine training mission. She was out now on SAR duty with Lieutenant Colonel Cecil Sams, USAFR, in command. Her position was well north of Fairbanks and considerably to the east of the direct flight path from Elmendorf to Point Barrow. Because of the panoramic visibility available from the flight deck of the C-119, all six members of her crew had a fine view of the ground below. The Flying Boxcar was an excellent aircraft for this type of mission because of her unusual visibility and because, being propeller-driven and piston-powered, she was low and slow. In a eyeball-type search mission these were desirable characteristics.

Colonel Sams talked directly with Elmendorf and got the message—there was a peculiar radar contact approximately sixty miles from his present position; it was requested that he investigate. The C-119 dropped one wing, turned, and headed off to the specified location. As soon as he was on the new heading, Colonel Sams notified the two pararescuemen on board that the aircraft would be in the vicinity of a possible survivor contact in approximately twenty minutes and to be be prepared to jump.

To these men, this was excellent news. To them, their parachutes were vehicles, extremely convenient for stepping out of airplanes at a variety of altitudes and arriving on the ground a short time later exactly where they wished to be. Between them they had logged more than five hundred jumps and they were thirsting for more.

Colonel Sams had no real reason to suspect that the radar blip would prove to have anything whatever to do with the lost party for which he and his crew were searching, but the call came from rescue center and anything of an unusual nature merited close attention. He did not dismiss the idea that the downed aircraft might have been flyable and was now once more airborne, although he could not visualize how they had been able to start the engines after a more than forty-eight-hour cold soak. Whatever it was, Colonel Sams was fully prepared to deal with it as required.

Three minutes later, the pip disappeared from the watching

radar screens. It did so because Andy hauled down the kite and weighted it with stones to be sure that it would not blow away on the ground.

"By this time they should have seen it if they are going to," he said to John in explanation. "Later on we'll fly it again. If it keeps appearing and disappearing, they may be a lot more curious than if it just appears and stays there."

"Would there be any radar covering this region?" John asked.

"You can bet your hat on that. Alaska is a prime defense area. A lot of the top Army brass feel that if we get into another major ground war, the arctic will be one of the big battlefields. The Russians, for instance, are expert in cold-weather operations. And Alaska is the key to the whole North American continent. You could lose Texas in it, and it has the smallest population of any state. Add it up."

"So that's why there's so much Army and Air Force up here!"

"You're getting the message. Say, do you hear an airplane?"

John listened for a scant moment. "Andy, I think I do!"

In less than a minute Jim Hill, who was checking on the condition of the air marker, waved his arms in the air and jumped up and down to attract attention.

"He's heard it too," John shouted, his voice rising in his excitement."

"Go tell Captain Gregory, fast!" Andy directed. "I'll try to get the signal fire started." He set off through the snow as fast as he could manage, but he had not gone more than thirty feet when the sound of an approaching aircraft was clear and loud in the sharp cold air. One moment the sky overhead was a clear cobalt blue from horizon to horizon, then the air shook with the sound of engines and a C-119, flying at not more than two thousand feet, swept into view over the top of a low ridge.

It was the most magnificent, wonderful, thrilling sight that any of those who beheld it on the ground had ever seen.

Jim Hill almost turned himself inside out trying to attract attention where he stood, but he could have saved his energy. The brilliant air marker, which had been colored with the sea dye from the life-raft survival kit, was all that was required. The twin-boomed aircraft flew over, turned, and then made a lazy circle of the area. After that it retreated for a minute or two, turned, and made one more pass at low altitude, rocking its wings as it did so. By now all of the men who had been in the snow cave were outside and although the effort was futile in the still strong arctic wind, they let out a considerable cheer.

It was rescue, and they all knew it. John, out of breath but hopelessly excited, came panting back to where Andy stood and pointed to the sky. "It's a C-119, isn't it?" he panted.

"Right," Andy answered. "The good old Shuddering Henhouse. There aren't any in the Air Force any more, so that must be a reserve outfit."

"Do they know what they're doing? I mean, as well as the regular Air Force does?"

"You bet," Andy said. He watched as the C-119 swept around in one more big circle and then began a pass slightly upwind from the center of the shallow valley.

"Watch for parachutes!" Andy warned. "They may be dropping supplies, or the rescue boys may be on board. If they are, they'll be with us shortly."

John watched, fascinated, but not quite knowing what to do. He did not feel cold, he did not even notice the wind, as he kept his eyes toward the C-119 in the sky. He even forgot the cardboard sunglasses which he was wearing and which worked surprisingly well despite the limited vision which they permitted. For a moment he saw a black spot materialize at the rear of the podlike fuselage, then a shape left the aircraft, and within a second or two, a long streamer of silk appeared behind it. The silk popped open into the form of a large round canopy, and now he saw the clear figure of a man dangling below in the harness. A second chute followed. As the plane flew on by, the effect was that it had laid two colorful Easter eggs in the sky.

The parachutists were experts, as all pararescuemen are. The first one touched down less than ten feet from the center of the air marker, while his partner, who had jumped after him, landed within fifty feet of the wrecked aircraft, which was now almost entirely obscured by drifted snow.

As though he were doing nothing more remarkable than parking a bicycle at the curb, the first jumper pressed the instant, one-point release on his parachute and stepped free. He walked the canopy down until it was fully deflated and then turned to greet Jim Hill, who was close behind him. "Sergeant Meadows," he introduced himself. "Air Rescue Service. My partner is Airman Hester."

"Jim Hill, copilot. Believe me, we're mighty glad to see you!"

"That's what we're here for." He unslung a compact walkie-talkie radio from his back and pulled up the antenna. "There were eleven in your party, right?"

"Right."

"Number of survivors?" the sergeant asked.

"Eleven."

"All of you? That's phenomenal. My partner is a corpsman, he'll look after the injured immediately. The medical supplies will be dropped on the next pass."

"No injured," Hill reported. "One man badly frostbitten

because he made a fool of himself, but he's in better shape now."

The sergeant stared at him as though he could not believe what he heard. "First report," he said into his radio. "Copilot of plane reports all, repeat *all,* members of party survived the landing. Also no injuries; I say again, *no injuries.* Stand by."

He turned to Jim Hill. "Let's get to your people. And what do you need most?"

"We could use some blankets if you have them on the aircraft. And while we have rations, anything you could spare would be appreciated, I'm sure."

The rescueman again talked into his set. "Need blankets and rations. Send 'em down and stand by for head count." He turned to Jim Hill. "I don't want to sound corny," he said, "but I'd like to see your leader."

"This way," Jim replied, "follow me."

On the way to the mouth of the snow cave they met Airman Hester, who was with John. There were quick introductions as they approached the rest of the party. Overhead the C-119 made another pass, but no supply parachutes appeared.

Captain Gregory met the rescuemen and introduced himself. "Come inside where it's warmer," he suggested. "We can be much more comfortable there."

"What have you got, a snow cave?" Hester asked.

"A very good one, I'd say," the captain answered him.

"This I want to see," Hester said. "I know about them, of course, and theoretically I know how to make one, but I've never seen anything other than small practice models."

"You'll see one now, just crawl in through the tunnel."

The rescuemen did as directed, and soon all of the members of the party were inside the domed room cut from the heart of the huge snowdrift.

The sergeant looked about him. "This is one for the book,"

he said. "I've pulled a lot of people out of tough situations, but I've never seen anything as well done as this. All you need is a latrine to make it perfect."

"Just around the corner to your right," Andy said. "The reason we're not too badly off here is because everybody pitched in and worked hard. We have a pretty bad frostbite case, and you might want to take a look at him. We thawed him out with hot compresses."

"That's the only way to do it," Hester, who was the medical corpsman, said. While he bent over Morton for a detailed examination, Sergeant Meadows swiftly took a count of those present and then shook his head.

"I've been in the rescue business eleven years," he said. "On the basis of where you went down, the weather, the time of year, and what you had with you, I had hoped that we might be lucky enough to find two of you still alive. To find every one of you here, and only one man in anything like bad condition, is a miracle. You must be the best bunch of survival men I ever met."

Captain Gregory pointed to Andy. "There's your survival expert," he stated. "None of us were able to deal with what we were up against. He brought us through."

"You can say that again," Morton contributed. "I gotta hand it to the kid, he really did a job. Pretty smart for a boy."

Sergeant Meadows looked at him a little oddly and then turned to the others. "We'll get you out of here as quickly as possible," he said. "We don't have any choppers in the area, and we'd have to refuel them to get them up here, but we might make it with a ski-gear C-130. There are two of them at Elmendorf if they aren't out flying. By now they'll have the word that you've been found."

"We don't mind waiting a little longer," Captain Gregory

told him. "Actually this isn't too bad at all. We could use some food, if we can get some, and blankets would help out. Otherwise we can stick it out, particularly knowing that we've been located. Mr. Morton might need some medical aid. But how about you?"

"Oh, we're here to stay," Airman Hester answered. "We came down to help you out, and we'll be with you until you're airlifted out of here."

"Specifically it's part of our job to help you survive," the sergeant added. "But you need us for that like a kangaroo needs a baby buggy. Now I've got to go outside and report."

The rescuemen, accompanied by Andy, Captain Gregory, Jim Hill, and with John bringing up the rear, crawled back through the tunnel and looked up at the C-119, which was still circling overhead.

"Meadows," the sergeant said into his radio. "Head count of eleven confirms all personnel safe and accounted for. No casualties. One man, Morton, that is M-O-R-T-O-N, was frostbitten, but condition appears satisfactory."

"Understand all personnel safe, no casualties," came out of the set. "Will drop blankets and rations on next pass. Have some frozen meals; can you thaw out or shall we do it? Not too much holding time remaining."

"We can thaw out," Sergeant Meadows reported back. "Advise Elmendorf survivors have constructed snow cave, are comfortable and secure. Believe C-one-three-zero on skis can land here. Will check possible landing area and advise."

"In the next ten minutes, if you can," the aircraft radioed back. "Elmendorf specifically asks about boys in party. Condition report wanted."

Sergeant Meadows glanced at Andy and grinned slightly.

"Boys are fine. One is a survival expert, and he is responsible for good condition of party."

There was a pause and then the aircraft came back. "Supply drop in one minute near air marker. Request explanation radar echo noted from this area."

The sergeant looked at Andy and repeated the question. "We flew a kite with a piece of metal hanging from it," he answered.

The information was passed up to the aircraft, and then things began to take shape rapidly. Captain Gregory, who had been over the area on foot while laying out the original air markers, offered his opinion that a ski-equipped C-130 would have no great difficulty in making a successful landing and subsequent takeoff from the floor of the shallow valley. Two parachutes came down carrying a blanket pack and a quantity of rations. A second aircraft which had been on search patrol, this one a C-118, arrived over the area and asked if any more help were needed. As soon as it was on station, the C-119 Flying Boxcar departed, since its fuel reserves were getting low and its holding time had expired.

Some consultations were held by radio, using the walkie-talkie on the ground, the C-118 on the air over the area, and the rescue-control center at Elmendorf—Fairbanks acting as a relay station. It was agreed through this line of communication that, since the available daylight was already beginning to fade, no attempt at a night landing would be made and the survivors, plus the pararescuemen, would spend the night in the snow cave. With the addition of the blankets and much improved rations, no difficulties were foreseen, and something approaching genuine comfort might be possible. A medical kit was dropped containing frostbite lotion and other supplies which might be useful. A half hour later, when the C-118 flew away, it was the general feeling of all concerned that the rest of the rescue operation would be an easy matter. Morale was high in the snow cave.

It went even higher when the food dropped from the C-119 was heated and served. For all but the pararescuemen it was the first real meal any of them had had in more than two days. The little fire in the snow cave took an agonizingly long time to thaw out some of the frozen dinners, but Andy refused to make it any larger. "Snow melts," he reminded everyone. "If it gets too warm in here, the walls will start dripping heavily, and we might even have a collapse. It isn't worth the risk."

"You're dead right on that," Sergeant Meadows agreed. "It's quite comfortable in here, but it's still the open arctic outside, and that's something to remember."

By nine most of the men were asleep. Andy stayed up, since he had the fire watch, and he would not let the rescuemen relieve him. While the burden was off his shoulders now, with two survival experts on the scene, he still wanted to hold up his end to the finish.

It was past ten when Morton sat up slowly and heavily and looked at him. When he spoke, to Andy's utter surprise, he for once managed to keep his voice low. "I want to talk to you," he said.

"Go ahead," Andy invited.

"You don't know the reporting business," he said, his voice hoarse in his throat, "but it's tough; it's made that way."

Andy said nothing.

"I work for myself, so I have to push harder to get results, and that's what I've got for sale—push."

Andy laid a stick on the fire and then looked toward the big man once more. He still did not speak.

"Anyhow, that's why I have to be the way I am, you understand? Maybe you don't, but, anyhow, I realize now that you may have saved my hide for me, and I want to be man enough to say 'Thank you' for it."

"That's all right," Andy replied. "I was glad to do what I could."

"I'm going to make you famous," Morton concluded and lay down again.

Andy did not pay too much attention to that remark. For a long time he sat looking into the little fire that was still burning steadily and then poured himself a little hot tea. They were not out of the woods yet, and the morning could bring many unforeseen things.

10 *Homecoming*

Because the arctic days were now very short, it was not daylight until almost ten the following morning. Everyone was already up, and the hot coffee, thanks to Jim Hill and Sergeant Meadows, was ready in reasonable quantities. Apart from the fact that all of the men were unshaven, there was little to indicate the severe experience which they had all been through.

With the first sunlight there came also the throb of aircraft engines. A single C-119 made a run over the shallow valley, a parachute streamed out, and a jumper appeared swinging in the harness. Andy had a good view of him coming down; with Captain Gregory and Jim Hill he was helping to mark out a landing area for the C-130 which was expected in at any time. The parachutist made an expert descent and touched down only a few feet away from the work party. He folded his chute, gathered it up, and then came over. He was well prepared for his jump—his auxiliary chute was still rolled up in its chest pack, he had on full jumping gear, and in addition, an arctic face mask which had protected him during his descent. Now he removed it and looked at Andy. "Hello, son," he said.

"Hello, Dad!" Andy greeted his father. "I hope you weren't worried about us." He introduced his two companions and waited while greetings were exchanged.

"I would have been a lot more worried if you hadn't had all that good training in survival methods," Colonel Driscoll replied. "I take it that it paid off for you."

"It certainly did, Dad," Andy acknowledged. "Come over and see our snow cave."

"I want to do that. I've heard you have a good one. By the way, you're going to have lots of company this morning. A C-130 will be in to pick you up in a little while. Also we have a photographer coming to take some shots of the survival equipment you built to use in our future courses. We want to show the students that these techniques really work."

"I can vouch for that, sir," Captain Gregory interjected. "During the storm we had our situation was, at best, critical. If we hadn't had your son with us to show us what to do, I very much doubt that we would be anywhere nearly as well off as we are now."

"I'm glad he was useful," the colonel said. "How is the other lad?"

"John?" Andy answered. "He couldn't be better. Right now he's in the cave manning the hot-coffee detail."

"Did you say hot coffee?"

"Yes, sir—right this way."

Despite the fact that the weather was still well below zero, a warm and hearty atmosphere prevailed inside the snow cave. Everyone was aware that they would be on their way back to civilization by noon or a little after, and the feeling of optimism was high. Andy introduced his father to all of the party. "Great kid you've got there," Morton said, and the others reacted similarly.

"Two ski-equipped C-130's are coming in," the colonel announced. "The first one, which is due in about an hour, will pick you all up and take you directly back to Elmendorf. The second, which will be forty minutes behind the first, will gather up all of your personal belongings from the C-47, along with some other gear; it will be delivered to you later in the day."

Captain Gregory, who recalled vividly the condition of the cabin of the C-47 following Morton's rampage, looked at Jim Hill significantly. The copilot nodded back.

Preston Williams took the floor. "I'm sure the Army or the Air Force wants these blankets back," he said. "It might be a good idea to get them ready and down to the landing area along with anything else we will want to take with us." This started a general movement within the snow cave; Bernstein retrieved the short-handled spade which had been used to dig the cave. "If no one else wants this," he declared, "I'd like to have it as a souvenir. Unless it's government property, of course."

"I'm sure you can keep it," the colonel told him.

The time began to pass quickly for the stranded men. Three of them returned to the wrecked C-47 to see what could be done about putting the luggage in order. They solved the problem by packing the loose things into whatever suitcases were handy, with the idea that the personal property could be sorted out back at the air base. It was bitterly cold inside the downed aircraft, and after half an hour of work they returned to the snow cave to warm up. They were on their way across the snow field when the air was punctuated by the high, shrill whine of turboprop engines. Over the same ridge from which Colonel Sams' C-119 Flying Boxcar had appeared, a big C-130 burst into view and began to circle.

Out on the landing area the two pararescuemen, Captain Gregory, Jim Hill, Andy, and John were just completing the job of marking what in their judgment was the best available landing strip for the Hercules transport. The four-engined freighter made a low pass over the area, pulled up, circled, and dropped its ski gear down into position. Then the flaps came down, and it began an approach. To John it seemed to grow bigger and bigger as he stood well to one side of the place where it was expected to touch down. The air shook as it swept past him; a few seconds later its nose rose in a landing flair and then it was sliding across the surface of the snow.

By now everyone was out of the cave. Andy, however, accompanied by his father, returned to the massive snowdrift which had given them desperately needed shelter and carefully looked around him. Because he liked to do things right, he closed the latrine with a few shovelfuls of snow and then packed everything he had left back into his own compact survival kit.

"I don't think you'll need that now, Andy," his father told him. "It certainly paid off on this trip, but I guess it's over."

"I'm sure of that," Andy agreed, "but, still, even though those birds have four engines, something *could* happen."

Colonel Driscoll laughed. "You're right," he admitted. "I should be the last one to say anything against your survival preparations."

When they emerged from the cave, where Andy had, as his last act, carefully put out the little fire and made sure that no sparks remained, the huge freighter had taxied back and was standing, rear ramp open, in the snow.

Andy and his father walked down toward it in the still-sharp arctic cold and looked at the vast interior of the freighter. Some of the party were already on board. Morton, his face carefully covered against the cold, was escorted by Airman Hester. The loadmaster who came with the Air Force transport was supervising the comparatively simple job of getting everyone on board with the limited equipment which they had brought with them. "The troops will be in later to pick up the rest of your gear," he advised. "Our orders are to get you back to Elmendorf for a medical check as quickly as possible."

In twenty minutes the whole party was aboard the aircraft. Andy sat next to his father, with John on his right. Then, with a hydraulic whine, the actuators closed the two halves of the rear ramp door and the number-four engine began to turn. Few of the reporters could see out, since the fuselage of the airlifter had almost no windows. When number-three engine started spinning, the heaters came on and a welcome blast of genuine warmth began to fill the hold. Within five minutes the temperature was high enough to permit the men to discard their parkas and arctic hand coverings.

With all four engines lit and turning, the pilots of the turbo-prop went through the long and involved check list and then sent back the loadmaster to be sure that all seat belts were secured. The whine of the engines grew to a screaming roar and the plane began to slide forward on the snow. Despite the friction, it gained speed rapidly, skipped a time or so where the snow was not smooth, and then lifted its nose up toward the sky. Because it was lightly loaded in terms of its capacity, it climbed rapidly, made a steep turn toward the south, and was on its way.

The C-130 was much faster than the C-47 had been, and the ground underneath seemed to move backward with impressive speed. Since he was located up near to crew door on the left-hand side, John had a small porthole available; he twisted around sideways on the canvas seat which ran from front to rear and looked out. The weather seemed perfect, and the big aircraft was obviously covering the miles as only a modern plane can do. Fairbanks passed by underneath and then it was only a matter of perhaps an hour more before the waters of Cook Inlet could be seen ahead covered with a broken sheet of ice and the ice in turn by loose snow.

On the flight bridge communications were rapid and efficient. The C-130 was number two to land behind a C-135 jet arriving from the "south forty-eight" which was enroute to Tokyo. After a very brief delay, the C-130 lined up the runway, began to come down the glide path, flared, and touched down with the remarkable gentleness for which that type of aircraft is noted. It took another four minutes to taxi up to the same terminal gate from which the party had left only a few days before.

There was a considerable reception committee: Colonel Walton was there, some medical officers, operations officials, and the local press. One photographer was on hand; when Morton spotted him, he managed to maneuver into position to get his picture taken as he walked from the aircraft into the terminal.

When they were all gathered inside, Colonel Walton spoke to them briefly. "I know you all want to get to your quarters and clean up," he said. "But we would appreciate it if you would take the bus outside to medical for a brief checkup.

137

Then you'll be taken by staff car to your quarters, where you will be able to wash up and rest. I'd like to invite you all to be my guests at the O-club this evening, at eighteen hundred, where we'll have a solid prime rib dinner. I'm glad you are all back safely."

The medical checkup did not take long. Both the boys were found to be in excellent condition; they were discharged with the recommendation that they go home, take a hot bath, and then get some rest before dinner. This prescription was entirely agreeable, so within a few minutes they were back in Colonel Driscoll's quarters and getting out of their heavy arctic gear in which they had lived for more than three days.

"You know," John said, "I'm still trying to catch up with myself. Here we are, warm and comfortable, and yet just this morning we were stranded up near the Arctic Circle."

"I know how you feel," Andy answered. "Guys come through here, stop for a meal, and a few hours later they end up in Saigon or Bangkok. It's modern life, I guess. But there are a lot of areas left in the world where things are still wild and savage."

"I'd say we just left one. If we'd had to hike out, or come by dogsled, it would have been a long, hard pull. By plane it was almost too easy."

"No argument. Now go in and take your hot bath, I'll give you first crack. Leave me some of the hot water."

"Don't worry."

At six that evening the entire party assembled at the officers' club in response to Colonel Walton's invitation. The dinner was excellent, and there was much talk about the job which had to be done to unscramble everyone's personal belongings in the baggage which had been brought back. At first Colonel Walton had not been able to understand why there was so much chaos, so Captain Gregory took him aside and gave him a short briefing on what had taken place.

Preston Williams spoke for the group in acknowledging Colonel Walton's hospitality. He stood up and faced the others in the private dining room, freshly shaven and very unlike the bedraggled man who had emerged from the C-130 only a few hours before.

"Gentlemen," he said, "in view of its happy outcome, I for one feel that my life had been considerably enriched by the adventure which we have just been through."

"Hear, hear," Chick cut in.

"Thank you. For the first time in many years I did a real day's work, and I can guarantee you that until my dying day I will remember how we all labored together to carve out that snow cave and the greasy taste of the rations that were in the life raft. But don't misunderstand me, I'm immensely grateful for both. And while on the subject of being grateful, I want to propose a toast. I feel certain that every one of us here, excepting Colonel Walton and Colonel Driscoll, of course, is, at the least, profoundly indebted to the very capable, resourceful, and —I don't hesitate to add—outstanding young man whom it was our very good fortune to have as a member of our party. Thank heaven, gentlemen, he went to the right school and paid attention to his lessons!"

Immediate laughter followed that remark and then applause.

"So, gentlemen, I give you Colonel Driscoll's remarkable son, Andy Driscoll, who, as far as I am concerned, may very well have saved all of our lives."

Colonel Walton stood up and raised his glass. The other men of the party did so as well; the last to rise was Morton, who made a considerable effort, apparently, to get out of his chair.

"Andy Driscoll," Bernstein pronounced. The men drank and then sat down.

"Andy, we'd like to hear from you," Colonel Walton said. His words were followed by applause.

Reluctantly Andy got to his feet. "I'm just lucky," he said, "that my Dad is an Army officer, which gave me a chance to get those lessons you spoke about. But, seriously, I wish that everyone could learn something about survival. The way people travel these days it can be Alaska today and Saudi Arabia day after tomorrow. There's a lot of open territory—jungle, ice cap, desert, and ocean—in the world, and all of it is hazardous. You never know when you might be suddenly down somewhere and then a little knowledge can go a long way. Thank you."

There was applause again, and Andy flushed. John gave him a playful poke and whispered, "Now that this is all over, what are we going to do for excitement?"

Colonel Walton took the floor once more. "Gentlemen, I understand that some of you are going out on the eight ten flight to McChord, and that the rest of you are manifested on the nine forty to McGuire. In view of this, I suggest that we break it up here and go down to the terminal. I have some staff cars waiting outside."

In the lobby the men reclaimed their gear and filed into the four waiting sedans which Colonel Walton had provided. Morton, however, hung back and waited until he was the only one remaining and so able to ride down to the flight line with the colonel himself. He climbed into the car and seated himself heavily on the plastic-covered seat. As soon as the car was in motion he turned to his host. "I was glad to see it work out that way," he said in a voice much too large for the small car. "Letting the kid get all the credit and so forth."

"I understand that he deserved it." Colonel Walton looked at his guest to see what was coming next.

"Oh, the kid was all right, so let's leave it at that. But just between you and me, that isn't quite the whole story."

"Isn't it?"

"Nope, it isn't. You see, when we were forced down, everybody was in pretty much of a panic. Gregory didn't know what to do and said so. We were all confused, no leadership. Now I've got a pretty loud voice and I can make myself heard. So I stood up and told the boys that somebody had to be a strong leader and I figured that I was the man."

"Indeed," Colonel Walton said.

"That's right. So I took charge and pepped the boys up with some real life. I can truthfully say that I was the last man to seek shelter and I suffered for it—you can see my face."

The colonel didn't say anything. He remained silent until the car pulled up behind the others at the terminal. Morton climbed out first and claimed his baggage at the counter. Then he looked about him and saw that some of the Anchorage civilian press was in the terminal talking to various members of the party.

"Hello, everybody," he boomed in a voice that stabbed through the terminal. "I'm going out on the first plane, so if you want to talk to me, you'd better do it now."

Two men came over to see him. "Your name, sir?" one of them asked.

"I'm Morton, Gill Morton, you know my name, of course."

"I'm sorry, Mr. Morton, I'm not sure that I do."

"Well, you must really be behind the times up here in Alaska. You ought to know me, I'm the greatest free lance in the business, if I do say so myself!"

"I see," the reporter said in a voice a quarter the size of

Morton's attention-getting tones. "And what part did you play in this matter?"

"Well, I don't want to draw too much attention to myself, but you might say I was the leader of the party. One thing's for sure, I'm the man who stayed outside and watched for rescue airplanes while the others were making themselves comfortable in that hollow snowdrift."

"Oh, it *was* hollow! I understood they had dug it out themselves."

"Oh, they dug it out all right. It wasn't much of a job, a little snow shoveling, and with a break every ten minutes for hot coffee, they were in good shape. But somebody had to be strong enough to stay out there and take it, to signal the rescue planes whenever they came over. That called for a strong man and I was the strongest in the party. So that's how it was."

"How did you plan to signal the planes, Mr. Morton?" The question was formally put, but the interest had gone out of the words.

"Lots of different ways! You ask Andy, that kid over there, and he'll tell you. You probably wondered about my first name; my mother's name was Gill, so I got named after her. That's Gill Morton, and the world is my beat—I go everywhere. Why, only last year—"

"I'm sorry, Mr. Morton," the reporter cut in, "I'll just have time to get back and file copy. I know you'll excuse me."

The reporter retreated quickly, and then Morton noticed that his companion had already left. A loudspeaker system came on and announced the fact that the flight for McChord Air Force Base near Seattle was ready for boarding. With a flourish Morton picked up his luggage and strode to the doorway. Then he set his bags down, turned, and waved.

"Well, so long, guys," he boomed. "It was great having you

with me, all of you. You sure made up a fine team. So long, see you in the headlines. So long, Curly."

Colonel Walton, who answered to that nickname in the presence of his intimate friends, winced inwardly as Morton strode out the door. No one said anything until the big man was safely on board the aircraft and out of earshot.

"And I thought he had straightened out a little," Andy said, a little bitterly, to his father.

"That kind never does," Colonel Driscoll answered, his arm across his son's shoulders. "But remember this—he didn't fool anyone but himself. Back where he comes from he'll probably tell everyone that he was the great hero, and a few may believe him. But the world is a small place within the ranks of one profession. The truth always comes out in the end. Don't worry about him."

"He's an awful loudmouth," Andy complained.

"I know that, son, and so does everyone else around here. He won't be invited again; and around the Army, if everybody is suddenly too busy to see him, he'll probably blame his tough luck. He's his own worst enemy; leave it at that."

Together father and son started to walk out of the terminal. Knowing what the colonel must have been through when his only son was lost somewhere out on the open tundra, John hung well behind to give them this time together.

And then the terminal building suddenly came alive. A red light in the corner began flashing, and the loudspeaker system came on with sharp crispness. "Attention, all military personnel . . . report to your duty stations immediately. This is an alert, repeat, this is an alert. It is not a drill. It is not a drill."

"So long, son," the colonel said and was quickly out the door.

John stood in the terminal, not knowing quite what to do.

Then Andy joined him and said, "We might as well stay here. You'll have a good view of what goes on, and when the first rush is over, we'll be able to get a ride of some kind back to my house."

Outside men clad in heavy parkas were running around, but each of them seemed to know exactly what he was doing. From somewhere down the field the roar of jet engines began to build up. Then, accelerating down the runway, an F-106 interceptor began its takeoff run. It created a shattering wall of sound as both of its engines let loose the screaming thunder of maximum power plus afterburners. It seemed to John that it would never break loose from the runway, but close to the end it finally rotated and began to climb into the sky. It was followed by another and then another.

A formation of three fighters took off together, two of them side by side and the third close behind them. As they rose and disappeared, back of each could be seen the fiery interior of their engine tailpipes.

"There's a lot going on," John said, almost reflectively.

Andy stood beside him, looking out the window. "You're only seeing a tiny bit of all that is really happening. All over this whole state the Army and the Air Force are reacting the same way. If the Navy has anything around the coastline, they're fully informed too."

"How long will it take for the word to reach down south?" John asked.

"It happened just about the same time that we heard it here. As soon as something was detected that justified an alert, the word was passed to NORAD, that's the North American Defense Command, and NORAD notified SAC, the Pentagon, and the whole works."

"So they all know."

144

"They sure do—right now."

They had to stop talking as another string of jet interceptors made their takeoff runs and climbed into the sky. Fire and crash equipment was out on the ramp and ambulances moved into position, each bearing the red Geneva cross which marked it as a mercy vehicle.

"How serious is this?" John asked. "Do you think it's the real thing?"

"At this point I doubt if anybody knows," Andy answered. "All I can tell you is that somewhere something was picked up. It may have been the DEW line, or it could have been BMEWS [Ballistic Missile Early Warning System] over at Clear." He pointed to a picture on the wall. "Each of those three radar antennas is a lot bigger than a football field and they have tremendous power and range—the radars, I mean."

"So this could be it!"

Andy was calmer and less disturbed. "It could be, of course —that's why the alert is in. But the chances are better than a thousand to one that it's a false alarm. But up here we don't take any chances. This is the first line of defense, you see, and that's what makes this whole state so tremendously important."

"Alaska," John said, and let the name hang in the air. "I can't believe it all. It used to be just a word to me, a frozen place up north somewhere that didn't mean very much. Now all of a sudden I feel very different about it."

Andy turned toward the exit. "I think we might get a ride back now," he said. "The first reaction is over and the all-clear is due anytime. If it's going to come, that is."

John stepped outside behind his friend, felt the chill in the air, and looked up into the night sky. "It's cold," he said, "but a lot warmer than where we were."

"After a while," Andy answered, "you grow to like it. You trust your parka and the rest of your gear. I guess it's like skin diving; with the right equipment you can go places where you couldn't otherwise, what the Army calls a hostile environment. But I don't think of Alaska as hostile. It's a wonderful place, and someday it may grow in ways nobody has thought of yet."

Together they began to walk, the snow crunching sharply under their feet. Andy was calm and assured, and John, beside him, began to feel some of the same spirit. "I've seen a lot of Western movies," he said. "About the frontier, the desert, hostile Indians—things like that. That's all history now. But it just occurred to me that Alaska is a bigger frontier yet. You don't have Indians—"

"Yes, we do," Andy interrupted, "lots of them."

"I didn't know that," John answered. "Anyway, instead of the tribes on the warpath you have the severe cold, but it must be better in summer."

"It is. It gets warm up here just like the banana belt, that's what we call the southern tail of Alaska. Up in Fairbanks they always have a baseball game on the Fourth of July that starts right at midnight. The sun is up, of course."

"Everything's different in the arctic," John commented. "But it's beginning to get to me. I wish I could live up here the way you do."

Andy looked up to watch the trail of a returning jet. "I guess we're all right this time," he said. "But you never know."

"I've just thought of something," John cut in. "I've got a name for Alaska. It's the last home of adventure."

Andy slapped him on the shoulder. "You're right about that," he agreed. "It could be a battlefield, but whatever happens, this is the place with the future. You take a look at your

Los Angeles and then take another up here at the arctic, and you'll know."

He pressed his lips together in a confident smile and then pulled the fur of his parka about his face.

"It's getting colder. Let's look for that ride," he said.

"Fine," John answered. "I'm getting the idea too! I want to see more of the arctic. Let's go."